The Infinitely Stranger Cases of Sherlock Holmes

by Paula Hammond

Edited by David Marcum

© Copyright 2025
Paula Hammond

The right of Paula Hammond to be identified as the author of this work has been asserted by her in accordance with the Copyright, Designs and Patents Act 1998.

All rights reserved. No reproduction, copy or transmission of this publication may be made without express prior written permission. No paragraph of this publication may be reproduced, copied or transmitted except with express prior written permission or in accordance with the provisions of the Copyright Act 1956 (as amended). Any person who commits any unauthorised act in relation to this publication may be liable to criminal prosecution and civil claims for damage.

All characters appearing in this work are fictitious. Any resemblance to real persons, living or dead, is purely coincidental. The opinions expressed herein are those of the author and not of MX Publishing.

Hardcover ISBN 978-1-80424-679-5
Paperback ISBN 978-1-80424-680-1
ePub ISBN 978-1-80424-681-8
PDF ISBN 978-1-80424-682-5

Published by MX Publishing
335 Princess Park Manor, Royal Drive,
London, N11 3GX
www.mxpublishing.com

Cover design by Awan

Table of Contents

The Devil's Snare	4
The Case of the Ghazi Genie	42
The Case of the Bryniau Witch Tower	68
The Case of the Covent Garden Medium	103
An UnChristian Act	135
The Violated Grave	165

Also by Paula Hammond 'Eliminate The Impossible'

"gentle wit, genuine warmth, suitably gothic elements...The author excelled in the depiction of the characters, accompanied by solid research. Overall, this is undoubtedly one of the finest single-author collections of traditional pastiches that I have read recently."

GoodReads

"These stories are the real deal: Holmes and Watson in the correct era, investigating Canonical-style cases."

David Marcum

The Devil's Snare

Holmes was lounging in his armchair, busily packing his before-breakfast pipe with all the dottles left from the previous day's smokes. I had just rung for breakfast and was contemplating my own pipe of Ship's when Mrs. Hudson materialized at the door.

Our landlady was an eminently practical woman who had come to accept her home being invaded by all manner of strange characters with almost saint-like serenity. That morning, however, she looked so sorely tested that both myself and Holmes immediately leapt to our feet. "Why," I asked, "whatever is it?"

"You'd best come see for yourselves," she answered, "and, Doctor, bring your bag, I'm afraid you may have need of it."

Although it was still early, that morning was one of those bright days when summer hadn't yet given way to autumn. The hallway was illuminated by a shaft of sunlight streaming through the fanlight, and it was this which made the figure lying on the floor look as though he was carved in marble.

On closer examination, the prone youth was revealed to be dressed entirely in white. A mane of black hair framed his face, which looked curiously flushed. His body was rigid, his hands tightly clenched, and while he was fair-faced, he had a pinched and terrible expression, which was made all the more horrifying for way his eyes stared, unblinking, at the ceiling.

His pulse was fast and irregular, his pupils dilated, and it was these final details which gave me my diagnosis: *Epilepsy*. Fortunately, I was familiar with Trousseau's work and, while medicine is still woefully uninformed as to the causes of the *grand mal*, I was relieved that I could at least treat its symptoms.

I loosened the poor fellow's tie, removed his collar, and tried my best to make him comfortable, placing my own jacket beneath his head as a makeshift pillow.

For a moment, it seemed that the catatonia would pass. Then the youth's body began to shake and spasm with such fearful violence that I feared he would injure himself. Thankfully, the epileptic paroxysmal didn't last, and Holmes and I were soon able carry him up to our rooms. There, we drew the blinds and lay him on his side, on Holmes's bed, to recover.

Holmes had often spoken dismissively of the fairer sex, but he always exhibited a great courtesy to them in person. "My dear Mrs. Hudson," he said, in the gentlest of tones, "you've had quite the shock. Please, do sit down and tell us everything."

Our redoubtable landlady would only acquiesce once she had furnished us with that great British cure-all – a pot of tea – after which she settled into Holmes's favourite chair to relate the morning's events.

"I was preparing rashers and eggs for yourself and the Good Doctor when I heard someone at the door," she said. "The bell rang in a series of quick, sharp *dings*, so urgent-seeming that I dropped what I was doing and fairly ran to the door. When I opened it, there was a young man standing there, a cigarette in one hand, the other still on the bell pull.

"I don't think he saw me at all – his attention was quite elsewhere. He was straining to look at someone or something over his shoulder, so that when I asked if I could be of assistance, he almost jumped out of his skin.

"He spoke quickly, in a breathless tone that spoke of great urgency. He asked if this was the residence of Mr. Sherlock Holmes, and when I said that it was, he asked to be admitted.

"All the while we spoke, he continued glancing over his shoulder, as though there was someone he wished to avoid – someone who was fast on his heels . . . ."

"Did you see anyone?" Holmes interrupted.

"No, but the young man was on the top step, which quite obscured my view of the pavement below."

"Excellent, Mrs. Hudson. Please, continue."

"He was nervous – jumpy I'd say. I felt sure he must be in grave danger, so I wasted no time in asking him to step inside.

"He was almost in the hallway, still glancing back, when he threw up his arms and let out the most horrifying cry. His head spun 'round and he fixed me with the most awful stare.

Oh, Mr. Holmes, what a look he had! As though he had seen the Devil himself.

"I can tell you, I closed that door as fast as I could, throwing the bolt for good measure. I was just turning to speak to him again when I saw him shudder, then topple over. He dropped like a stone, and with such force that I heard an almighty crack as he hit the tiles. He looked so pale, I was convinced he had done himself a serious injury. He will be all right won't he, Doctor?"

I was reassuring the dear woman when, as if on cue, Holmes's bedroom door opened and out walked our visitor, looking a little ragged, but considerably less wan than he had half-an-hour earlier.

In another life, Mrs. Hudson would have made an excellent nurse. Within ten minutes, all three of us were seated around a roaring fire with a fresh pot of coffee and plates piled high with those neglected eggs and rashers. Within fifteen minutes more, we were replete – our visitor sore-headed and a little embarrassed, but otherwise well, and keen to relate his tale.

"My name," he began, in a soft voice, softened further by a gentle Cornish burr, "is Christopher Angove. I was orphaned when I was five and raised by my maternal uncle, Captain Pengellys.

"My Genni is soon to come into her majority, and we are planning to marry." Here Angove paused, and added in a defiant whisper, "Oh, the doctors have quite different ideas about that, of course! They would have me dosed on bromide and heading for a life of lonely solitude. But my uncle has always wanted the best for me – and my fiancé is quite prepared to take the risks of an epileptic for a husband.

"No, Mr. Holmes, despite the rather sad spectacle I've presented this morning, my life isn't that of the invalid. It is as rich as any young man could hope for – and about to be enriched further by the addition of a loving wife and, if the Lord blesses us, a family.

"However, the reason for consulting you has nothing to do with any of these things . . . . ." Here Angove faltered. "Before I go further, Mr. Holmes, I must ask you something. It will no doubt seem curious, and it may color your perception of me in the asking of it. But ask it I must, for the events I am about to relate occasion a certain flexibility of mind that isn't usual. My question is this: Do you believe in *devils*?"

"I have met real, flesh-and-blood men to whom I would happily apply the epithet '*devil*'."

"I mean Biblical devils, Mr. Holmes. Physical incarnations of evil."

If Holmes thought any less of our visitor for his question, he didn't show it. Instead, he answered in the same measured tone he often used with clients. "Why do you ask?"

"Because I am bedeviled, Mr. Holmes! Even now, even here, on the streets of this great metropolis, I am not safe. I'm being hunted, Mr. Holmes! Hunted!"

"I believe in *facts*, Mr. Angove" he answered. "Eliminate the impossible, and whatever remains, no matter how incredible it may appear, will be the truth."

"So, you admit the possibility?"

"I have no evidence to either prove or disprove the existence of what people call devils. So, yes, I would admit the possibility."

"And have you, Mr. Holmes, ever seen a devil?"

Holmes paused, his eyes twinkling mischievously. "If you mean a creature from the fiery pits – You would not credit it, but in my youth, I actually went in search of such a being."

Angove looked sufficiently intrigued for Holmes to elaborate.

"When I was a boy, it was rumored that a creature of great age and malevolence roamed the grounds of my school. It was said to walk the dormitories every evening, and if you weren't a-bed by lights out, it would appear and drag you off."

"Heavens!" I said, momentarily entranced by the unexpected revelation from Holmes's past. "What a tale to tell to young boys!"

"Indeed," Holmes smiled demurely. "The story was well established by the time I started as a boarder and, like all good stories, it was based on verifiable truths.

"The school was once a monastery which had been gifted an area of woodland by the King in the Twelfth Century. The land was said to be the abode of a demonic beast, whose lust for blood was so fierce that the King believed only God's influence would calm it. Apparently it failed, for the woods took on an ominous reputation. It was claimed that those who entered them would surely die.

"By the time the monastery became a school, there had been enough unexplained deaths in and around the area to make the woods off-limits – but that didn't stop boys from daring each other to spend the night there. The year before my arrival, two boys had gone missing. When they were found, they were quite out of their minds . . . ."

"Holmes!" I cut in, shooting a glance at our ashen-faced guest.

Holmes gave me the whisper of a smile before replying, "Oh, I think the young man is quite recovered, but you're right. That is a story for another time. Please, Mr. Angove…". Holmes waved a hand airily, for our visitor to continue.

"Kit," Angove said. "Call me Kit. Everyone does."

"Well then, Kit, tell us about your devil."

"It isn't so much my devil, as St. Mawr's. The legend goes back centuries – although I hadn't heard it until Skipper Williams told it to me."

"And who is Skipper Williams?"

"Genni – my fiancé's – father. He's in the same line as my uncle."

"Fishing?"

Kit raised an eyebrow, quizzically.

"I recognize a fisherman's calluses when I see them" Holmes explained.

Angove was tall and well-built, and now that Holmes had identified him as a fisherman, it was easy to see how the work and the elements had fashioned him into the fine young man he was.

"My uncle has a small fishing fleet" Kit continued. "Nothing too grand, you understand. Six boats, which has given him income enough to school me and make me an allowance – which I rather waste on clothes!" He blushed, chuckling at his own expense.

"Uncle still thinks of himself as a humble fisherman, but he spends as much time behind a desk these days as he does at sea. I help him when I can, as he intends for me to take over the running of things, in time. As I say, he has never considered me an invalid. 'Fresh air and exercise – that's the ticket!' he's always said."

"If I may," I interjected, "how long have you been afflicted by these seizures?"

"Since I was a boy. My uncle believes they stem from my parents' accident. They died when their carriage overturned. I remember nothing of the tragedy but, since then, the fits have come on me in times of distress, so my uncle may have the truth of it."

"When your parents died," Holmes asked, "were you left anything in trust?"

"I see where you are going, Mr. Holmes," Kit replied, with an fresh edge to his voice. "No. My parents were barely starting out in life. All they had was each other. And all my uncle had was his beloved little sister. He's always cared for me as if I were his own."

"And this devil?"

Kit took a deep breath, steadying himself it seemed, before replying. "They call it 'Old Tebel'. He's said to haunt the hills around St. Mawr's. He latches onto young men and carries them away on their wedding night."

"For what possible reason?" I asked.

"To protect Cornish maidens from unsuitable beaus!"

Holmes barked out a laugh.

"I agree, Mr. Holmes," Kit said, quietly – as though somehow the creature he spoke of could be conjured just by the saying of its name. "Any other time, I would have been laughing along with you. But this thing is real. You must believe me!"

"It followed you here?" Holmes asked, leaning out of his seat, in an attitude of intense concern.

"The truth, Mr. Holmes? I've begun to see him everywhere. Never fully, you understand. Just glimpses. A shimmering shape, something in the mist, half-formed, half-seen. But so unnerving that terror has begun to weigh upon me like an anchor. I fear I am losing my mind."

I had a sinking premonition that the young man's nervous system wouldn't stand up to a recitation of his encounters with this mysterious creature, but Kit was determined to persevere.

"I'm fine, honestly, Doctor," he said to my expressions of concern. "Let me tell you what I came to relate. Then, you and Mr. Holmes can decide if my troubles are worthy of your attentions."

Holmes pushed a glass of brandy into Angove's hand. The young man took it gratefully, downed it in one swallow before closing his eyes, and continued.

"I've known Genni since we were children. Her father used to work a lugger on the Atlantic Fleet out of Falmouth. He would be away for weeks at a time, and Genni's mother would send her out to ramble the hills to get her from under foot. We spent many-a-summer together climbing trees, fishing, and paddling – and had plighted our troth to each other long before we knew what the words meant.

"Genni's mother died before we reached adolescence, and my Uncle Jacob offered her father a job, so that he could be closer to home.

"Over time, our friendship grew into something more significant and, when I finished school, I didn't think it forward to ask for her hand in marriage.

"Genni isn't yet twenty-one. We cannot marry without her father's permission. Alas, he will not give it – feeling that a young man like myself, with little experience of life, may come to regret marrying so young. 'A childhood companion,' he says, 'is quite a different thing to a wife. And what you take for love may be nothing more than the natural affection that children, raised almost as siblings, have for each other.'

"In faith, I cannot be angry at his decision. Genni is his only child. His caution is natural. And he hasn't been unfriendly. Ordinarily, he's a quiet sort. Keeps himself to himself. Genni is his cook and housekeeper, and the two of them live very simply in his little cottage by the bluff. Yet, he has thrown open his home to me – and I have become a regular at his table.

"It was one evening, a week after my proposal, that it happened. I had been invited for supper. After, as Genni busied herself in the kitchen, her father and I took a circuit of the garden. The skipper passed me his cigarettes, and we talked of the future, with me I impressing upon him my good prospects, in the hope that he might relent and agree to our marriage sooner rather than later.

"After a while, the evening turned cold – a storm was coming and I had already begun to shiver – so we retired to the sitting room to warm ourselves in front of the fire. The weather quickly turned from bad to worse. Soon, the wind was howling down the chimney and rattling the casement windows so that, even in the cozy room, we felt its effects.

"I remember, as the evening grew darker, I found myself feeling strangely detached. The lights from the lamps and fire seemed too bright. I sunk back into the chair, into the dark, pulling a blanket around my knees. It was while I was in this queer frame of mind that Mr. Williams suggested a round of storytelling – the storm seeming to lend itself to tales of weird and wild things.

"I should, perhaps, have cried off, but he was in a rare good humor and I was keen to spend as much time in Genni's company as I could."

"'Here's tale you should appreciate, young buck,' he said, laughing, 'though mayhap you won't appreciate it quite so much once I'm done! Old Tebel has lived in these hills for longer than there have been people to tell of it,' he commenced.

"'*Tebel* is a Cornish word for the Devil – at least that's what my old Ma told me, for that's what the monster is said to look like: Tall, red-skinned, with clawed hands, and hoofs where its feet should be. His head is wreathed in fire, and he has a set of large, milky eyes – for he lives in the dark places and, like all creatures of the night, has great, saucer-like eyes with which to pierce the veil.

"'Now, the Tebel has a fancy for young girls, and it's his greatest joy to watch them. He never reveals himself to them but, oh, they feel his regard, of that you can be sure. He's there when they walk the wooded vales, there when they splash across the brooks and streams, there whenever they're out, in the lonely places. It's the Tebel who makes the young girls uneasy as day turns to night. It's the Tebel who makes them jump at shadows. It's the Tebel that makes them speed up their tread, although there's nothing to be seen beyond the gloom which grows ever thicker, ever darker.

"'In all of its unnaturally long life, the Tebel has never harmed a girl or a woman. No. You might say he feels proprietorial about them. As though these beautiful young creatures are his, and his alone. And it's there that the danger lies.

"'For while Old Tebel is content to creep and peep, to watch and lurk, should one of his young maidens appear with a beau, then bloody murder is the result.'

"While the tale was harmless enough, the more the skipper spoke, the more uncomfortable I began to feel. The light still hurt my eyes, and swaddled in my nook, I began to imagine that I was, in fact, ensconced in some deep cave, and instead of Williams sitting across from me, there was Old Tebel. I do not lie when I say that I saw the skipper's face begin to shift and remold itself into the form of a hideous demon. So strong was the vision that, in the grip of it, I unknowingly, cried out."

"'Oh, now Tás!' Genni jumped up. 'Enough of that!'

"Her father – *Tás* is her pet name for him – looked unchastened. Indeed, he seemed delighted at how well his ghost story had been received."

"'The Tebel is neither fast nor stealthy,' he resumed with a chuckle. 'You will hear him come for you. You will hear his hooves on the road, behind you. You will hear the *snicker-snick*, as he sharpens his claws. You will feel his fiery breath on your neck, and when you turn around, you will see him in all his demonic glory. Redder than arterial blood, burning with an unholy fire, and in his huge eyes, you will see your own reflection. You will see how you blanch as he moves towards you, and you will watch, paralyzed, unmoving, unable to cry out, as he hoists you onto his shoulder and carries you away!'

"I should, perhaps, have recognized the signs of an oncoming seizure, but it came upon me so quickly I barely knew what was happening.

"When I awoke, I was back home with my uncle. Beyond a dreadful thirst, I was well, yet I could remember nothing of what had happened – and I haven't felt at ease since."

"Have you seen this Tebel again?"

"Many times, Mr. Holmes. At first, whenever I visited my dear Genni, but increasingly, he seems to haunt my every movement. Why, this morning, as I was walking from the station – enjoying the sights of the city – I suddenly felt his baleful gaze. By the time I reached your door, I was convinced that I was about spirited away!

"Yet what is worse, Mr. Holmes, is that every time the old devil appears, the *grand mal* assails me. Each fit is more terrifying, more violent. After the last attack, I was insensible for many days. It was then that I determined to break it off with Genni. But oh, Mr. Holmes, if you have ever been in love, you will know that the heart and the head aren't always in accord. Instead, I have chosen the path of the coward. For this past month, I have kept my distance. We write to each other three times a day and, yesterday, came the most wonderful missive.

She declares that her love for me has only grown in intensity and, when she comes of age, nothing will stop her. We will marry – devil or no!"

"If I may ask, Kit, why did you think to consult Mr. Holmes? Forgive me, but demons are hardly his usual stock-in-trade."

"It was at my uncle's insistence. I had set out yesterday to speak to the skipper. Going against her father's wishes doesn't sit well with me. I still believed I could persuade him – and I wasn't disappointed. He said that time had proved me faithful and, seeing how miserable his Genni had been, he no longer has any wish to keep us apart. He gave us his blessing, although he wouldn't let me speak to Genni then – He wanted to give her the good news, and claim a little credit back for himself after being cast as the villain for so long.

"I was so giddy that I immediately went to tell my uncle the news. To my surprise, instead of sharing my joy, he insisted instead that I set out for London – there to seek you out and engage your help."

"He's clearly a perceptive man" replied Holmes in that quiet, intense way he has when a case begins to consume him. "Very perceptive. Now, Kit, I think Doctor Watson would prescribe bed rest – and plenty of it."

Angove didn't take much persuading. Holmes led him back to his own snug, little bedroom, leaving the two of us alone to plan.

"What do you think?" I asked. "Do you think there's a case here buried under all the monsters and myths?"

"I do. So far, everything I've heard screams foul play. I've no doubt that Mr. Angove is in deadly peril. But I must not ignore the possibility that this devil – for want of a better word – is *psychosomatic*. What do you think, Watson? Is he a reliable witness?"

"Is Christopher Angove really seeing devils, or merely imagining them, you mean?"

"Quite."

"It's hard to say. Throughout history, epileptics have been regarded as insane, half-witted, possessed. The Romans believed the illness was contagious. Until recently, it was said to be caused by sexual excesses. Many of those attitudes persist. Even in England, in the enlightened nineteenth century, you will find epileptics refused work, condemned to the workhouse, or worse, to an asylum, because of a misunderstanding of the illness. Those who enter such institutions rarely leave. All I can say with any surety is that we have no idea what we're dealing with."

"Perhaps a better question, then, would be: Could his visions be caused by the epilepsy, or should we seek some outside force?"

"The mind is a curious thing, but from what little I know of epilepsy, if visual or auditory hallucinations occur – and it is rare – then they occur *during* the seizure, not before."

Holmes stoked the fire and, for a while, we sat in silence. Then he finished his abandoned before-breakfast pipe, fixed his cool, grey eyes on mine, and said "What we have heard is very suggestive, but we must step cautiously. Watson, I have never needed you more. I will be relying on your knowledge and good sense to guide me."

With those words, I suddenly felt a great weight fall upon me. I only hoped that I was equal to the confidence Holmes placed upon me.

St. Mawr's nestles on the southern coast of Cornwall, looking for all the world like a picture book painting of how an English fishing village should be. A long, straggling street fronts the sea and, along it, runs a row of picturesque cottages, painted in breezy blues, pretty pinks, and sunny yellows.

A pier stretches out from the sea wall, affording a fine view of the remains of a medieval castle on the peninsula. The castle itself is a surprisingly squat and ugly thing – which, as many visitors have commented – quite spoils the otherwise idyllic scene.

The region owes its prosperity to a flooded valley which was carved out during the Ice Age and now forms one of England's largest natural harbors. It is in this harbor that St. Mawr's fishermen ply their trade. And it is in the wooded hills above the village that those who have made their money in that most perilous of occupations build the homes.

Cornwall may be known as the English Riviera, but the journey to Saint-Tropez is considerably easier than the one we took from London to St. Mawr's. A hansom, a sleeper-train, and a steam ferry were necessary to reach the village itself. An open carriage was awaiting us on arrival and, after a long and weary journey, it was a delightful to have the fresh sea-breeze on our faces as we were whisked through the village and up, into the hills, beyond.

Captain Pengellys's home is known as *Dowr Carrek*, which is Cornish for *Rock Anchorage* – and the age-worn, angular grange turned out to be a wonderfully suitable place for the square, much-weathered sea captain.

The driver had barely brought the horses to a halt when a berry-faced hulk of a man appeared. He lolloped, ape-like, towards the vehicle and, before we could protest, he'd taken our bags and was heading back towards the grange, calling for us to follow.

Pengellys may have been a man of some standing locally, but his home was a place of domestic simplicity. There were no armies of servants – just a cook and a maid who came from the village "to do for the captain". They shared his table and his confidences as though they were family.

Holmes, whose Bohemian soul railed at the straight-jacket of society, was quite charmed.

As soon as we had refreshed ourselves from the journey, we were invited into what the captain called the back parlor for a glass of mead and some saffron cake.

A pair of French windows opened out from the parlor into a walled garden and, while Pengellys attended to some household duties, we took the opportunity to explore. The garden was a sprawling affair, filled with all sorts of nooks and hideaways that would have been delightful in the summer. This late in the year, it was sorely overgrown, with only the hardiest of plants still in bloom.

Holmes made a beeline for a foul-smelling broadleaf, with striking, trumpet-shaped flowers.

"Look here, Watson," he said, in a tone of suppressed excitement.

"Interesting?"

"Very. This, my dear Doctor, is the infamous *jimson weed*. A poisonous plant from the nightshade family, it's more commonly known as *The Devil's Snare*. It's found far and wide – often in coastal areas. Its seed pods get scooped up with ship's ballast, or washed and blown onto foreign shores. It's also become a popular curio with travelers who bring it home, intrigued by the tales they hear of the plants more unusual qualities."

"Oh?"

"Oh, indeed! Originally, shaman used the flowers to induce visions. Ingested, they cause delirium. In large doses, they bring on fits, madness. Even death . . . ."

Before I could question Holmes further, we heard Pengellys's voice from the parlor, calling us in. Kit had been instructed to help Mrs. Harris in the kitchen, allowing us to talk freely with him while his young ward was otherwise occupied.

"I asked Kit to engage you because I know that something is very amiss," he began. "It seems to me that someone has it in for my boy. I can see no rhyme nor reason for it but, in the last year, Kit has become a shadow of himself. I begin to fear for his life, Mr. Holmes, and that's no lie."

The big man's keen, dark eyes traveled from Holmes to me, and back again – and my companion appeared to be appraising the captain in much the same way.

"You don't believe in this Old Tebel, then?"

"It's rot, Mr. Holmes. All this talk of devils and demons! I'm a Christian man, so perhaps I shouldn't be so quick to dismiss the possibilities, but I can think of better things for one of Old Nick's creatures to do than haunt lovestruck young men."

"Tell me about his epilepsy" I interjected.

"We have never hidden Kit's illness. On the contrary, I've been sure that it was known so that should he be taken bad, those around him would know what the trouble was and how best to care for him."

"And generally, how often do the fits come upon him?"

"Why, never Doctor."

"Never?"

"When he first came to me, he had a very hard time of it. But good Cornish air, and the feeling of being useful – that's all a man needs to grow up strong. Until this Tebel business, he hadn't had an attack for seven, eight years – more even. It was my belief that he had outgrown it."

"Is that possible, Watson?"

"It's widely held that fresh air and hard work is beneficial. And those who are stricken as children do sometimes recover as adults," I affirmed, not feeling anywhere near as confident as I sounded.

"Has he ever had hallucinations – visions – before?" I continued, trying to get a feel for Kit's symptoms.

"When he was a child, he swore for months that his mother was watching over him. But I couldn't tell you if it was the grief or the illness at work."

"And when the fits resumed, did you notice anything different about them?"

"They appear with no warning, are more violent, and take a greater toll." The captain sighed sadly.

"Mmm." Holmes steepled his fingers together and regarded Pengellys intently. "You said that you felt someone might 'have it in' for Kit. Has he any enemies?"

"Hardly! I may be partial, but the boy hasn't a bad bone in his body. Why would anyone take against him?"

"What about yourself, Mr. Pengellys? Any business rivals?"

"Psh! This isn't London, Mr. Holmes. I'm a fisherman. My neighbor's a fisherman, my neighbor's neighbor is a fisherman, my housekeeper's husband is a fisherman. The only thing anyone gets hot under the collar about here is the size of their catch. Besides, at sea, your life may depend on the man next to you. Grudges get themselves worked out pretty fast in those situations."

"Your domestics?"

"Mrs. Harris and Elowen, you mean? They've been with me this past year, since my old housekeeper retired. Came with good references from Falmouth."

"Didn't Williams used to ship out of Falmouth?"

"He did. What of it?"

"Just following a train of thought, Mr. Pengellys. Do they tend the garden?"

"I do it myself. I rarely have the time to keep on top of the weeds, these days – though why you should be asking about that, I'm sure I don't know," he added, sounding irritated at what he must have taken for random queries.

"What about Williams?"

"Man's an odd fish, but he owes me his livelihood. His daughter is about to become my daughter. What grievance could he have?"

"Indeed." Holmes said, his eyes glinting. "Do you have any suspicions?"

"Nothing more than my guts telling me Kit is in terrible danger. But look, I've been speaking to Mrs. Harris about supper this evening. I haven't sent out the invites yet, but I was thinking of asking Williams, Genni, and some of the other skippers. Give the dog chance to see the rabbits?"

"That sounds ideal, Mr. Pengellys. Now, if you'll excuse me, I'm of a mind to take a little constitutional. Tell me, are the boats back yet?"

The captain glanced at the clock on the mantel. "Not for a couple of hours. They'll come in with the tide."

"Excellent! Perhaps I can take that invitation round to Miss Williams, then?"

The captain gave Holmes a sly, knowing smile, looking considerably warmer towards him than he had a few moments earlier.

"Watson?"

"Yes?"

"You don't mind staying here?"

"Not at all. Truth be told, I'm still a little fatigued by the journey."

"Then look to Kit, and ensure he isn't left alone with anyone outside of the family."

"Lord!" Pengellys exclaimed. "Is it that bad then?"

"It may be nothing at all," Holmes said. "Time will tell, Captain. Only time will tell."

Pengellys may have considered himself a humble fisherman, but he certainly knew how to host a splendid supper.

Holmes and I were to be guests of honor, and it appeared that everyone who was anyone had come out to give the "gentlemen from London" a good looking at.

Despite that fact that Pengellys employed at least half of the twenty people seated around the table, the conversation was refreshingly free of attempts at affectation or flattery. The captain often found himself the butt of the joke – and gave as good as he got, with no indication of bad blood.

The young lovers spent much of the evening glancing at each other, clearly oblivious to anything else.

The captain kept the drink and conversation flowing with an enviable ease, although it didn't escape Holmes's notice that his glance was often towards the couple.

Most of the talk was, as the captain had warned us, about catch sizes, which appeared to be a topic of endless fascination. Only once were voices raised. Yet even then, it seemed like the rehashing of age-old grievances, rather than real malice.

"Any minute now," Kit, said to me, conspiratorially, nodding towards a jowly, blancmange of a fellow, busy filling his face, at the end of the table. "Three glasses down, and he's about to start at it."

"You're a good man, Jacob" the florid-faced skipper suddenly said, raising his voice to be heard over the general mur-

mur of table-talk. "God knows, I don't begrudge you your success, but how can one man, with one boat, hope to compete with you and your six? Should I come home empty handed, I can't send out another boat to try their luck elsewhere. Should I hit a good patch, I can only take what will fill my hold."

Kit leant over and whispered, "He does this every time, Doctor!" The complaint seemed so well-known, it was followed by a chorus of, "Hush, Lowen!" and groans of, "Not this again!"

"I won't be silenced! Lowen barked back, waving a fork piled high with slices of roast beef, like some ancient battle standard. "You can fill six holds, while I go hungry!"

"*You* go hungry?" a voice chipped in from the end of the table, which occasioned much laughter. "That's a new one!"

"So, that's how it is?" Lowan cried, his face, purpling even more. "You invite me here to be mocked!"

"Come now," the captain said placatingly. "Five times in the last month, my fleet has turned home empty, while you've hit gold. Luck is either with you or not. My offer still stands. You can come out with my boats – we'll work the fields together."

"I'd rather be my own boss, thank you," was the sullen reply.

"You know full well that Cadan often puts out with us. He's still his own boss."

"Psh! For now. But I know what you're about, Jacob. You want to buy up every boat out of St. Mawr's."

"Rot! Seas are rich enough for us all to share! Come, fill your glass, refresh your plate. We're all friends here."

Lowen did, indeed, return his attentions to his plate, after which the table returned to its good-humored chat.

I was seated beside Kit and Genni, who seemed well-suited in every respect. Kit was tall and broad-shouldered. Genni was almost as tall, and brown as a berry. Where Kit was dapper in his choice of fashion, Genni's clothes were simple but tasteful, her long, black hair worn down and unadorned. When she spoke, it was in a sing-song voice, full of joy, and free of artifice. London society would have had no time for her, but I was quite enchanted.

Skipper Williams had been placed beside Holmes, allowing my companion to easily get the measure of the man without seeming to pry.

Williams proved to be taciturn, initially speaking only when spoken to. It took all of Holmes's considerable charm to thaw him out at all.

"You must be looking forward to the wedding, then?" I heard Holmes occasion.

"As much any father looks forward to losing a daughter," was Williams's morose reply.

"Surely, you aren't so much losing a daughter as gaining a son?" Holmes teased.

"Oh, you must take no notice of an old man, set in his ways, Mr. Holmes," Williams said, lightening his tone. "Genni is my only family. Of course, Kit would be a fine catch for any young woman."

The evening progressed in much the same way, with neither Holmes nor myself hearing anything that pointed at deeper resentments towards the captain or the young lovers.

Within a few hours, the party began to break up, the fisherman being keen to get some rest before the early tide drew them back to their boats.

Holmes and I had retired for a glass of port with the rest of the stragglers, and were exchanging notes on the evening, when Holmes suddenly grasped me by shoulder.

"With me, now, Watson! If I'm not mistaken, we are about to reach the end of the game."

Despite the evening chill, it appeared that some brave souls had ventured outside, for the French doors were now ajar.

I followed Holmes outside where I saw Kit and Skipper Williams, walking towards an ornamental gazebo, deep in conversation.

I took Holmes's lead, moving cautiously along the wall, using the shadows and soft grass to mask our approach.

"Well, then, my lad, it's all agreed," I head Williams say. I saw him reach into his pocket to pull out what appeared to be a cigarette case, which he offered to Kit. "I think we've time for a celebratory smoke before we head indoors, don't you?"

Williams struck a Lucifer. As the match caught, its phosphorous glow illuminated both men in a blaze of white light and I was momentarily transfixed by the look of utter hatred emblazoned across Williams's face.

I didn't hear Kit's reply for, in a flash, Holmes was beside him, with myself practically falling over my own feet to catch up.

"Ah, there you are, Kit!" Holmes said nonchalantly. "The young lady sent me out to find you. I'm sure the skipper won't mind if I share a cigarette with him instead?

Without waiting for a reply, Holmes whipped the cigarette out of Kit's hand, and leant forwards to light it on Williams's match.

If Angove was bemused by Holmes's rudeness, he didn't stay around to comment, for the news that his lady had requested his presence was enough to send him rushing indoors.

"Interesting," Holmes said, regarding Williams cooly. "Can't quite place the blend."

"I really couldn't tell you," Williams responded, sounding uneasy. "Picked them up at the port. They aren't my usual."

"Really? They look home-rolled." Holmes pulled enthusiastically on the cigarette, blowing little smoke rings in the skipper's face. "It has a strange scent, but I'd warrant Watson would find it less noxious than my usual mix."

The fisherman coughed and began to back away. "Well, I must be going," he stammered and, with that, he hurried for the French windows. "It's getting late."

"Why don't you see our new friend out, Watson," Holmes said airily, still drawing on the cigarette with an attitude of beatific calm.

I did as asked, recalling Holmes's insistence on not leaving Kit alone.

By the time I reached the parlor, Williams and Genni were the only remaining guests.

If the skipper had seemed self-conscious during supper, he was now in a state of intense agitation. Without a word, he grasped Genni by the elbow and fairly dragged her from the room. I watched them leave and, with a nagging but undefined sense of foreboding, I raced back to the garden.

I was at the windows when I heard a dreadful cry – so loud and tortured that my skin went cold and the hair on my arms began to bristle. I ran then as I had never run before, stumbling in the dark over penchants, fountains, bell jars, and all sorts of garden ornaments, in my eagerness to aid my friend.

The garden seemed impossible to navigate. In the gloom, I found walls where there should have been none. Bushes seemed to throw themselves under my feet. Rose thorns became barbed wire enclosures that plucked at my flesh and tugged at my clothes. And through it all, I could hear Holmes howling, like a man possessed.

Almost as suddenly as they began, the cries stopped, and I felt my blood run cold. I staggered on, feeling dreadfully afraid, until finally, my outstretched hand found the cold metal of the gazebo. Remembering the last time we were here, I fumbled in my jacket for my matches and, after several attempts, one ignited.

Holmes lay no more than a few feet from me – his long frame curled into a fetal ball, his breath coming in rapid gasps.

As I got nearer, I could see his flushed checks, mouth twitching, his pupils, so large and dark, that they quite consumed his face. He threw up his hands, coving his eyes against the flare of the match, with an audible groan. "Holmes, what is it, man?" I asked. "Can you speak?"

For a moment he seemed to shake off whatever had him in its grip. I saw a flash of recognition blaze in his eyes, and raising one hand like a twisted claw, he motioned me to come closer.

I knelt beside him, placing my ear to his mouth. He made a sound somewhere between a sob and a choke, then speaking with a feverish energy, he said "Red as a beet, dry as a bone, blind as a bat, mad as a hatter."

He shuddered again, his long hands, grasping at the night air, his eyes frantic. "Red as a beet, dry as a bone, blind as a bat, mad as a hatter," he repeated. The delirious refrain went on for many minutes, and with such intensity, that I began to fear for my friend's sanity. Then, I reminded myself that this was Sherlock Holmes. Regardless of appearances, there was some part of his remarkable mind that was trying to tell me what had happened.

I tried to question him once more, but it was clear that Holmes had quite exhausted what reserves he had. He let out one more heart-rending groan and, pointing to some horror which only his own disordered mind could see, he slipped into unconsciousness.

With the captain's aid, I made Holmes as comfortable as I could. Beyond that, there was nothing else to be done – and I fell back into anguished watchfulness.

It seemed increasingly clear to me that Williams was to blame for whatever had befallen Holmes. I kept re-playing that scene in the garden, over and over, in my mind. The cigarette – it had to be that. Yes! When we had first met Angove, Mrs. Hudson had said he was smoking. Holmes had been unable to find the cigarette. Then, I had wondered why he'd looked for it. It now seemed beyond doubt that there had been some toxin in it – and in the one Holmes had just ingested – that had been intended for Kit.

The Captain shared my instincts, along with a burning need for action. So it was, with Kit watching over my friend, that we headed out into the early morning to confront the skipper.

When we reached the bluff, we discovered a small crowd gathered around the little cottage. A pall of smoke hung in the air. With it came a cloying, fetid odor, that caught in the throat and made the eyes sting.

The captain jumped down from the trap, with a look of thunder on his face. "Williams?" he demanded. "Where the devil is Williams?" Pengellys buttonholed one of the bystanders. "You! What goes on here?"

"Seems the skipper lit a bonfire in the garden before he sailed," the man replied. "Damn fool left it smoldering. Would have had the whole house aflame if it wasn't for the neighbors raising the alarm."

The captain was in no mood for small talk, and neither was I. What was left of the cottage door lay on its hinges and the burly man pushed his way into the house, following the tracks of water and footprints left by the impromptu firefighters.

Apart from some smoke, the cottage was undamaged, but the small garden was a blackened mass of tangled and half-burnt foliage.

"What the Hell do you think he was about, Doctor?"

"Covering his tracks" I hazarded.

Pengellys bounded upstairs, calling for Genni, but found the place deserted.

"He could have taken her with him?" I suggested.

The captain ran his hands through his thick hair, tugging at his curly locks in frustration. "Damn it, Doctor, I've known this man for decades!"

We appeared to be at an impasse when a cry from outside sent us rushing for the door.

Genni, barefooted and soaked to the skin, was running across the road. The captain took flight toward her and, before long, he had swept the young girl off her feet and into his arms, holding her with all the protective instincts of a papa bear with its cub.

"Calm yourself, girl, calm yourself!" he said to the sobbing woman, but she was quite overwhelmed.

"Come, Doctor!" Captain Pengellys cried, carrying her to the trap. "Let's go home. It looks like we have another patient for you to care for."

The events of the last few hours had clearly taken their toll. On the trap, Genni fell asleep in my arms. It was fully twenty-four hours before either she or Holmes awoke – thankfully, both very much recovered.

We were gathered in the parlor, with the blinds drawn at Holmes's request, and it was there, in the unnatural gloom, that he related a tale whose details were as dark as the room itself.

"It was the story of Old Tebel that sparked my interest," he said, his voice cracking. "Was Kit such an invalid that a ghost story would send him into a fit? I didn't think so. Indeed, I tried one of my own, and even in his weakened state, Kit showed no signs of alarm at it. No, the story of Old Tebel was intended to create mischief. Or sew the seeds of some.

"Still, Watson had told me that epilepsy was poorly understood – and I felt on unsteady ground. Then, I learned from the captain that Kit had quite outgrown his illness . . . and that changed everything.

"Let us imagine that someone wishes to do harm, using a toxin that will induce hallucinations and bring about fits, safe in the knowledge that the effects will be taken for epilepsy. Let's imagine they throw in a tale of devils for the disordered mind to feed on. Very quickly, the *who* and the *how* becomes clear.

"There are many toxins that cause fever, delirium, tachycardia, mydriasis – a dilation of the pupils – even hallucinations. Only one, to my knowledge, causes all of these, plus a dreadful thirst and pronounced photophobia – *Datura stramonium*. The symptoms can be summed up by this jolly little ditty: *"Red as a beet, dry as a bone, blind as a bat, mad as a hatter."*

Holmes rummaged in his jacket pocket and pulled out a handkerchief. Inside was a crushed, white bloom which I recognized immediately.

"Jimson weed!"

"Quite."

"Why, Mr. Holmes," the captain stated, "I have some of that in my own garden. It grows wild over these parts. It's an insidious weed. I've spent many a day trying to eradicate it."

"I had noticed," Holmes smiled. "As you say, it's common enough. My visit to Williams's cottage revealed that he had his own quite-splendid jimson weed plant – Only, unlike yours, his was well cultivated, with signs of regular clipping.

The plant blooms late in the year, but his plant's flower heads were already quite gone."

"But good Lord!" Pengellys cried. "Why!"

"I kept asking myself the same question. What good is the *who* and the *how*, without the *why*? The only possibility was the marriage. So determined was Williams to prevent it that when the young couple vowed that they would press ahead regardless of obstacles, he set out to put an end to it once and for all."

"You mean – ?" I asked, aghast.

Holmes nodded grimly. "The cigarette I ingested was enough to lay me out for twenty-four hours – "

"You knew!" I cried.

Holmes held up a hand, placatingly. "The flowers could have been placed in Kit's food or drink, but that wouldn't explain his fit in Baker Street. The more I heard, the more I believed that the cigarettes Williams had been giving him held the secret. Nothing was certain, beyond the fact that, if I was correct, the risks to me were minimal. But to Kit? After months of being dosed with cigarettes, Kit was already, as the captain noted, a shadow of himself. I believe had he ingested that last dose, then madness or death would have been the final result."

"But why?" asked Kit, horrified.

"I think" Holmes said gently, "that Genni can tell us that."

The young girl sat on the floor beside Kit, looking so unlike the happy, confident young woman of the party that my heart went out to her.

"Mr. Holmes is right," she said. "I always knew that Tás was reluctant for me to marry. It is the way of fathers, I think. No man is ever good enough. Not even – " she glanced at Kit sadly " – the boss's son. But it wasn't until last night that I realized the hatred he bore for Kit.

"After we returned home, he was like a man possessed! He swore that no daughter of his would be 'sullied by a union with a mentally deficient'! I've never seen him like that. The way he snarled, the way his face twisted – it was as though I was looking at Old Tebel himself!

"Then he began pulling up the plants and building that terrible pyre. I was so fearfully afraid of what he might be about that I ran to the one place I knew he would never find me – the sea caves. You remember them, Kit? How we played there as children?

"He was so wild, so crazed, that he didn't see me leave, but later, I saw him, running along the sand, calling my name. I have never been so afraid. He railed and screamed and cursed, pounding through the surf until I became convinced that he would wake the whole village with his ravings. Indeed, a couple of fisherman, readying their boats for the tide, accosted him and asked him what he was about. For a moment, I thought he would recruit them to his cause, but instead he headed off, towards the cove where our own boat is anchored."

To hear such a story, to learn how one man had been twisted by hate until all reason was gone, shocked me to my core. Williams had lost everything – family, home, livelihood – and he was now a fugitive. And why? Ignorance, half-truths, and fear. "Good Lord!" I cried, feeling a deep despair creep upon me. "So that's it? He's slipped away then?"

"Don't worry, Watson. We can inform the authorities. Put the word out at the ports."

"Oh, I don't think that's necessary" the captain avowed. "If he went out with his crew, it won't be long before they'll be chomping at the bit to come home. If he didn't . . . Well, he'll soon have to put in. No skipper, no matter how skilled, can navigate Cornish seas on his own. It's just a matter of time."

"But what if he gets away?" I cried, feeling that some redress was necessary.

"What if he does?" Captain Pengellys proclaimed. "Good riddance! At the end of days, there'll be a devil waiting for him right enough – but it won't be Old Tebel. For now, I can consider myself doubly blessed. I already have the son of my heart – and now I have the daughter too. This is your home now, Genni, and as soon as we can arrange a priest, we will make that official."

At that moment, I looked from Genni to Kit, and suddenly I felt a flush of hope. These young people had endured so much, yet their love had remained strong.

"This is what it's all about, aye, Doctor?" said the captain, beaming with fatherly joy. "We cannot stop the hate, but we can counter it with love."

"Indeed, Mr. Pengellys," I said. "Indeed."

NOTES

• Trousseau is Armand Trousseau, whose work covered what modern medicine would term neurological diseases, such as apoplexy, epilepsy, and Parkinson's Disease. He was one of the earliest physicians to describe *grand mal* seizures in detail.

• Bromide was an early treatment for the symptoms of epilepsy, and it is still used today. In the Victorian era, side effects could be severe, including skin blisters that could cause permanent scars, lethargy, slurred speech, uncontrolled body movements, and sexual disfunction. In Holmes's era, many of those with mild epilepsy preferred the fits to the cure.

• There is no St. Mawr's in Cornwall. We can only assume that Watson has changed the names to preserve the privacy of those involved in the events.

• Cornish folklore doesn't have any reference to an *Old Tebel*, although the word *Tebel* does mean *evil*. It is likely that Williams made up the story specifically to target Kit.

The Case of the Ghazi Genie

It was March of 1891. The stately carriage of time had not yet delivered me to the watery abyss of Reichenbach Falls. Nor had I any inkling of the portentous events in which my dear friend, Sherlock Holmes, was then embroiled. All I knew was that he had been traveling for many weeks, and I didn't expect to see him.

Holmes had been never one to write where a telegram would do. Indeed, when circumstances compelled him to put pen to paper, his letters were so short as to verge on uncivil, so infrequent as to make them useless as a form of meaningful *communiqué*.

That morning, however, I'd received a letter which was so out of character that, incredulous, I'd read snippets of it aloud to Mary, over the breakfast table.

It was gregarious missive, with many references to past cases, and much good-humored small-talk. "Why John," my wife said in *faux* alarm, "I think you should call Scotland Yard, for I've no idea who this man is who claims such familiarity with you. He certainly isn't *our* Mr. Holmes."

"Indeed," I laughed. "He's almost civil!"

Despite the humor of the situation, I found myself re-reading the letter over coffee looking – I confess – for some hidden message. If there was one, I entirely failed to see it, but I was left with the nagging feeling that something was amiss.

That feeling only increased when, in place of my usual eleven o'clock appointment, Holmes himself materialised, looking like a man stretched thin.

"As your waiting room is empty, I thought I'd avail myself of a few moments of your time. That is, if you can squeeze me in?" he asked in a tone laced with exhaustion.

"By Jove, Holmes!" I cried, propelling him towards a chair, for he looked ready to drop. "Are you quite well?"

"A little tired. I've been using myself rather too freely of late."

"I thought you were in Europe?"

"I was. Unexpected events have brought me back to England. I will have to go away again, soon – for at least six weeks. Perhaps," he added darkly, "infinitely longer. I'm sorry to land at your door unannounced. I still have much to plan, many possibilities to consider . . . Yet I'm sorely in need of my Watson. Why, do you know that it's ten years, this week, since we had our first adventure together?"

"So, that's what your letter was about!" I exclaimed, relieved that it was nostalgia, rather than anything more sinister that had prompted such a curious correspondence.

"Ah! I see – I've worried you?"

"No, no, not at all. Well, maybe a little. Mary's convinced you've been replaced by some nefarious *doppelgänger*. She's all set to bring in Lestrade to track down the real you!"

"Ha! Now, that I would like to see. The fellow couldn't find his own hat." For the first time since he'd arrived, I caught a glimpse of the Holmes I knew of old – glittering eyes, the whisper of a smile.

"I'm sorry to be the friend in need, Watson, but I'm sure my doctor would warn me that I cannot carry on as I have been – without any respite. What say you to a few days fishing? Perhaps Plymouth? We may have to make do with pollock or wrasse, but the weather has been mild of late. We may be lucky and bag ourselves some spring mackerel."

If I'd learned anything from Holmes during our long association, it was that often what someone doesn't say can be more significant than what they do. I couldn't have known that, even then, Professor Moriarty haunted his every step. I did know that my friend needed me – and I'd seen him wear himself weary with work too many times to refuse.

That day was Saturday the seventh. Sunday was a day of rest, giving me plenty of time to free my diary and arrange a *locum*. "If I clear my urgent appointments on Monday, I could be at Paddington for five o'clock, if that suits?"

"Excellent," Holmes said, suddenly jumping up. "I'll reserve a carriage on the 5:15. Now, I've intruded too much already. I'll arrange provisions. You bring the rods."

It was still an hour before sunset, but by the time I reached Paddington, the day had taken on a sombre aspect. The weather, which had been clear all week, had turned chilly and an untamed wind, tinged with the scent of snow, propelled me onto the platform.

It howled ominously across the station's great wrought-iron arches. Billows of steam, illuminated by electric light, formed a rippling aurora, turning Brunel's great monument into a cathedral of light.

I didn't know why, but there was something about the spectacle that put me in mind of my days in Afghanistan. Of a night-sky full of stars, of early morning mists, and the ruddy glow of guns guttering in the distance. I stood, trying to retrieve one particular memory for some minutes. Several times I thought I almost had it. Then, another gust quite blew it away.

I hurried on, shivering, thankful for my heavy Ulster and the carriage blanket, secured in my luggage. To think that I'd laughed at Mary for insisting I bring it, with spring just around the corner!

I've travelled a few times on the new City and South Electric-Traction Railway, and it may be that such modes of transport will soon be ubiquitous. Yet, for me, nothing beats the scents, sounds, and sensations of a steam train. The tang of coal-smoke in the air. The jubilant crow of the whistle. The heavy vibrations as the great iron beast gets up to speed. The rhythmic chug of the engine at full power.

I fought my way though the crowds, enjoying each and every sensation. My porter was less enamored of the spectacle, huffing like a miniature engine beside me, until he finally located our carriage. Holmes was already ensconced within, his pipe creating its own little steam-plumes.

I was relieved to see how relaxed he looked, and I mentally thanked Mrs. Hudson for the flush on his cheeks, which spoke of the benefits of good food and a well-turned-down bed.

As the train pulled out of the station, I noted that the weather had taken a turn for the worse. It was snowing in earnest now. Great globules battered the windows, and the wind veered so quickly from northeast to southeast that it quite obliterated the view.

The express can cover the two-hundred miles between London and Plymouth in less than four hours. Our more modest conveyance gave us five hours in which to sample the contents of Holmes's sizable hamper, which was packed with cheeses, potted meats, hearty cobs, shortbreads, Queen cakes, and, to my delight, small bottles of both port and brandy.

The windows were tightly shut, but the gale was such that, directly, we were compelled to close the ventilators and pack every crevice with wads of paper, torn from my notebook.

Soon, the temperature in the carriage had fallen so low that I was obliged to unpack my blanket. I was pleased to see that Holmes had brought his, and suitably immune to the chill, we settled down to enjoy the journey.

Our progress proved to be painfully slow. The rising winds and falling snow tested the train to its limits. It crawled along. At each station, we spent longer and longer lying in wait as, no doubt, the driver debated the prudence of pressing on.

Fortunately, our journey wasn't urgent. Indeed, we were merrily reminiscing over a pipe when, without warning, there was a deafening thud, like the sound of muffled ordinance booming in the distance. Immediately I had visions of Maiwand, of the guttering echo of nine-pounder guns, the leathery scent of black powder.

The vision quite stunned me. I sat, blinking, for some time, temporarily lost in the past. "Down, Watson!" Holmes cried, ducking low. There was another thud, followed by a strange, muted screech, as if metal claws were being raked along the side of the carriage. The curiousness of the sound shook me out of my reverie.

I quickly followed Holmes's advice, for it felt certain that we would be de-railed. Instead, the train teetered to one side, somehow righted itself, gave a great shuddering exhale, then stopped dead.

Holmes, still crouching low, edged open the blind, his keen eyes scanning the darkness outside with an air of nervous expectation.

"What is it?" I asked, looking at his taut features expectantly.

For some time, he said nothing then, eventually satisfied, he gave a great sigh of relief and unfolded his long, thin frame. "Forgive me, Watson, I'm jumpier than a cat. It would seem the weather has defeated us. We appear to be stuck fast in a bank of snow."

"Goodness, that came down quickly."

"And it shows no sign of abating" he said, still glancing out of the window, anxiously. I followed suit, but saw nothing but a blizzard of white, a pair of bobbing railway lanterns, and the echoing shouts of the driver to his fireman.

Soon, a third lantern joined the cabal. I watched their slow progression along the length of the train checking, I guessed, for damage. Then the little party headed back towards the engine, where I saw the glint of a coal shovel, accompanied in quick order by the dull grunts of the fireman getting to work on the drift that surrounded the train.

"It looks like they might try to dig us out. Where do you think we are?" I asked.

"Based on our rather pitiful speed, and the number of points we've passed, somewhere outside Exeter."

"Well, then, we've still plenty of time for a warmer. In the meantime, maybe you could put that brilliant mind of yours to work on a mystery that's puzzled me since my army days."

"Oh?" Holmes replied, suddenly rapt. "How is it that I've never heard of this mystery before now?"

"To be honest, I'd almost forgotten. There isn't a lot I do recall about Afghanistan. Perhaps I've tried to forget, for it's enough to feel the old wounds complain as winter closes in. I've no desire to pick at the scars. Still, there was something about that odd light-display at Paddington that set me thinking about the Khyber. Then, that noise we heard just before the train stopped – put me in mind artillery guns."

"It did sound rather explosive," Holmes commented, putting a strange emphasis on the last word. "Still, however long we're stranded, thanks to the ever-dependable Mrs. Hudson, we'll be well fed. So, here, take that little warmer, and tell me your mystery."

I took a glass of port, feeling rather pleased to have something with which to regale Holmes while we waited out the storm. But where should I begin . . . ?

We'd struck camp near Ali Musjid Fort, looking towards Peshawar, at the end of November.

It's a place that lies heavy with the weight of history. Arid, narrow, bounded by precipitous cliffs of shale and limestone. Kipling called it *"a sword cut through the mountains"*. In truth, it's so narrow in places that barely two camels can pass through, side-by-side.

The fort that guards the pinch-point of the Khyber Pass had only recently come under British control. The summits that surround it are less than four-thousand feet above sea level, but the cliff sides are near vertical. The result is a claustrophobic corridor where fast, low winds rise suddenly – just as the winds have done tonight. Only it's sand, not snow, that comes sweeping across your path.

We were a mixed bag: Baluchis, Gurkhas, Jats, Sikhs, Punjabi Muslims, Frontier Pathans, and a rag-tag collection of Brits.

Tensions were running high, for this was a spot where many young men had lost their lives. We'd neither seen nor heard the Ghazi, but that meant nothing. The hills were dotted with tunnels and caves, some natural, some cut by the Afghans to hide munitions and men.

It was in that mode – sensitive to the slightest sound or movement – that we made camp. The sappers set up our 'Park' where we stored the ordinance, while we pitched our tents further along the old river bed.

If I'd had any say in the matter, we would have pressed on. I already had several patients wasting away with diarrhea, and one man had been tied to scaling-ladder and whipped so badly by his officer that I feared he'd die before we got to the Field Hospital at Lundi Kotal.

We'd been in Afghanistan long enough to be well-versed in the trick of making and breaking camp. We weren't, perhaps, quite the well-oiled machine of repute, but it wasn't long before the hospital tents were pitched.

I was busying myself readying the beds when I heard a commotion coming from the direction of the Park. Shortly after, one of the officers arrived to report that some of the levies had bolted.

That wasn't an unusual occurrence. The levies were fine fellows, but had no particular interest in upholding British interests, at the expense of their own skin. And the Pass was a dangerous spot.

It wasn't exactly clear what had caused them to bolt, and soon all sorts of rumors started to circulate, as they tend to do in army camps. Finally, one of the boy drummers came running in.

Jimmy Johnson was an admirable young lad with whom I'd made an arrangement some months earlier: I was to supply him with slugs of chocolate, while he would ensure that I was kept abreast of camp news. "Those damn sappers have cursed the whole bloomin' camp!" he chirruped, wide-eyed.

It's a curious thing that, despite the horrors of war, the young lads who took the Queen's shilling somehow still managed to be boys – with all the capacity for wonder and credulity of their kind. "Really, Johnson," I tutted, "what nonsense are you spouting now?"

"Honest, Doctor!" he replied, holding out a grubby hand for payment. "The sappers 'ave been digging up bones all morning. Fousands of 'em."

"Oh? Whose bones?"

"The levies say there's a shrine nearby – they're Holy Knights or summut. They say now we've disturbed their resting place, the genies will come to punish us. So off they scarpered."

"Genies! Good Lord, Johnson," I sighed, exasperated. "How many times do I have to tell you that you can't believe every little thing you hear?"

"God's honest truth, Doctor!" he protested, stuffing squares of chocolate into his mouth like a cocoa-addicted python.

"Pssh! The deal was news, not gossip! Now away with you – I have too much to do to be listening to fairy stories."

I thought little more of it until the next evening.

By then, the wind, had begun to rise again. Towards the Pass, I could see dust-devils gathering, sucking in debris as they whirrled and bobbed along. Abruptly, the wind started to shriek, until it reached to an ear-splitting crescendo.

An older, more circumspect Watson would have stayed in his tent. I wasn't that man.

I'd arranged to dine with chums in the Park, and was damned if I was going to let the weather deter me. So, with my cinder goggles firmly in place, I headed off.

Even with a lantern to guide me, it was tough going. Stumbling all the way, I weaved through the storm, head down, barely breathing, until my foot hit something hollow, and I tumbled into a dusty little oubliette.

In truth, it was little more than a scrape, over which someone had pulled a piece of tarpaulin. Yet the more I struggled, the more I became entangled. I would probably have remained there all evening, rolled up like over-sized caterpillar, if it hadn't been for Sergeant Kelly's mongrel, whose eager barks quickly brought the sentries running.

Thus, feeling rather bruised and foolish, I was delivered to Lieutenant Henn's tent, where Corporal Michael Brennan was already installed, glass in hand.

We were sitting and drinking milk punch when I asked Henn, who was with the Royal Engineers, if he'd heard about the levies.

"I should say so! Half-a-dozen of them gone. The Captain sent riders out to track them, but they've found nothing. His worry is, if the fools get themselves captured by the Ghazi, who knows what information the beggars will squeeze out of them before they kill them?"

"Do you know what set them off?"

"We seem to have stumbled onto some burial pit – Hazara most likely. Caused complete chaos. Aside from the necessity of finding the time to rebury the poor blighters, we had to relocate the whole Park. It isn't just the levies who are spooked, either. None of the lads want to spend the night camped on top of a graveyard. Mind you, bones or no, this is an eerie spot. Strange quality of light. Lots of echoes. Shapes that shouldn't be."

"Oh?" I said, sensing that Henn wasn't quite telling everything he knew.

"Oh, no! I'm not fool enough to tell the resident quack that I've been seeing and hearing things!"

"Ghosts?" I prompted, topping up his glass.

Henn sighed. "Well, you didn't hear it from me, but some of the men have reported lights, strange noises. I thought it was likely musket shot or rifle sights, glinting in the distance, so I headed out for a recce.

"I was outside the Park, looking up towards the Pass with my field glasses. Damn strange – there was a moment when the mountain itself seemed to move. Now, khaki is just the right color to blend in with the dust around here, so I started thinking that maybe our missing levies were hiding out in the hills. Some of those fellows are like mountain-goats, and they know this place like the back of their hand.

"I headed closer to get a better look. There are a few trackways hereabouts, used by goat-herders, but there were no footprints. No tracks of any kind. Yet here's the thing: I was just about to turn back towards the Park when I felt the air move. Then, clear as day, I heard a voice say '*Marg sta paa intizar di.*'

"I tell you, I came-about pretty sharpish. If there'd been anyone around, I'd have seen them. There was no one. But do you know what '*Marg sta paa intizar di*' means? '*Death awaits you*'. Put the bloody willies up me – and that's the truth!"

"Little Jimmy Johnson is blaming genies," I laughed. "Perhaps we'd better search the camp for magic lanterns!"

Brennan and Henn, both being Irish, had something of a literary streak. "Not genies. *Djinn!*" the one said. "Nothing like what you read about in fairy tales."

"Quite right!" the other chipped in. "Invisible spirits, the locals say. Capricious, like the fey folk. You don't want to get of their bad side. Who knows what devilry they'll get up to."

Henn looked to Brennan, a mischievous gleam in his eyes. "Half the sappers have stories. Noises. Things moving in the shadows. Kit going missing. Objects being moved. I believe you've met Bobby" he added, chuckling. "He's normally a perky chap, but he's been skulking around camp with his tail between his legs, growling at nothing all day. That is, until he had to go out and rescue some idiot doctor."

"Nonsense. He's probably upset that no one would give him a bone! Besides, there you've said it: The levies have stolen what they could, then hot-footed it to the nearest village to sell it. Wouldn't blame them, the way the Captain's been riding them."

"Ah, the Captain's already thought of that. There's no sign of them along the usual routes. No way they could outpace a horse on foot, either."

"They'll turn up eventually" I said.

"Maybe they will, maybe they won't. Or maybe the *djinn* have spirited them away!"

"You can't believe that."

"Our dear doctor's a sceptic," Henn nudged Brennan, conspiratorially.

"Only one cure for that," Brennan answered, grabbing a lantern. "Come on! The wind's dropped. Let's take a look over by the Pass. See if we can't whistle you up a genie or two!"

I was still a young man, with a reputation in the regiment as something of a hot-head. It didn't take much to goad me into doing something stupid – which, heading out into enemy territory with two drunken Irishmen to look for genies, undoubtedly was.

It was a clear night, bright, silent, with stars such as one only ever sees in truly wild places – the same stars, it occurred to me, beneath which Alexander the Great had marched forty-thousand men into India, two millennia earlier.

It was that cold, epic vista, I think, which began to unpick our bravado. It was easy to feel small and lost beneath such a vast, timeless display. Soon, the gay chatter evaporated, to be replaced by cautious whispers.

By the time we'd reached Henn's goat-track, we'd all unholstered our weapons, suddenly sober, aware of the precariousness of our situation.

The path truly was a goat-track. It wove its way upwards, following the logic of an animal whose only concern was filling its stomach. It would veer, unexpectedly, towards this tasty shrub, or that patch of grass, with no concern for the steepness of the slope or the ease of passage.

Not being goats, we progressed fitfully, sending torrents of loose scree tumbling down with every tred.

Eventually the trail widened, straightening out towards what looked like a cave mouth. It was there that we found them. Six scattered corpses, surrounded by loot, their bodies positioned in such a way that they appeared to have died running from some unknown foe.

The Ghazi had a reputation for playing dead. I'd treated more than one solider with wounds inflicted by an apparently dead enemy, who'd miraculously returned to life to stab them the moment they'd walked past. Indeed, some soldiers had learned the habit of plunging a bayonet into any corpse they saw, just in case.

I wasn't about to follow suit. Besides, the levies may have been thieves, but we had no reason to suspect them of colluding with the enemy.

We inched towards the lonely clearing, revolvers at the ready, every step sounding like a pistol-shot, our breath echoing, thunderously. It seemed impossible that the enemy wouldn't hear us.

Still, we advanced. Still, the corpses in the clearing remained corpses – yet such corpses as I'd never seen before.

Symptoms of cerebral concussion showed themselves in their bloodshot eyes. There was blood, too, around their noses, indicating a rupture of the sinus and a fatal effusion. But there were no scalp wounds, no cuts, gunshot wounds, or lesions of any kind. If it hadn't been for their pallor, which looked so uncanny, paired with those crimson eyes, they might well have been asleep.

"How strange," Brennan said. "We haven't had any artillery drills."

It seemed an odd statement, for clearly none of the men had been hit by shot.

"Damn! Personally, I'd much rather have stumbled across a couple of *djinn* in these hills than this pitiful sight" sniffed Henn. "Come on – we can send a work party out later to collect the bodies but, discretion being the better part of valor, I suggest we make double-time back to camp. I think you'll agree, gentlemen, that one unpleasant encounter this evening is more than enough."

Two hours later, enlivened by a pot of strong coffee, I carried out what would be my first autopsy.

Every student doctor learns his craft in the dissecting room. In spite of that, my career thus far had been preoccupied with the often Herculean task of keeping frail humans alive. In times of war, it's a messy process, largely devoid of emotion – for the doctor who pauses to worry loses lives.

An autopsy is an entirely different affair. There's no sense of urgency. The spark that gives us life has been extinguished – yet one must still give the dead their dignity.

I knew nothing of the body before beyond a name, which time has now sadly erased from memory. Even so, I recall readying myself to make that first incision, aware that here lay – first and foremost – a man. I owed it to him to discover what had killed him and, if possible, ensure that those responsible were punished.

What I found puzzled me then, just as it puzzles me now. His internal organs showed signs of massive trauma. Indeed, his insides had almost been liquidized. Organs, blood vessels – exploded. His brain matter was little better.

Had the man come to me, fresh from the battlefield, I would have expected to see the outward signs of such inward injuries: A crushed skull, or broken ribs. He had neither.

I examined one of his companions, keen to ascertain if his injuries were unique. They were not.

I had no answers. I couldn't conceive of anything that could have caused such catastrophic damage without leaving any signs on the victims' bones or skin. Nor did I have the luxury of time to research the puzzle further.

The next day, we struck camp, heading for Lundi Khan. The next, we were for Basawal, then Barikab, then Kandahar, and on.

My life quickly became one long routine of route marches, making camp, striking camp, fire, fury, blood, bandages. Until, that is, the Battle of Maiwand . . . .

Holmes refreshed our glasses. For a moment he regarded me in silence. "My dear Watson . . ." he whispered.

"I know," I said. Further words were unnecessary.

He nodded. "Well then, let us see what we can make of you mystery." He closed his eyes, steeped his fingers, and began.

"We will never know if the levies were genuinely spooked by the discovery of the bones, or simply used it an opportunity to vanish through the Pass with British kit to sell. The events you relate do suggest a certain level of planning, sparked, no doubt, by the discovery of the burial pit.

"It would seem that the levies took advantage of the confusion in camp to steal what they could, hiding their loot in little dugouts around the Park. It would have been a simple thing to wrap items in lengths of tarpaulin, dump them in a hole, and retrieve them later. It's likely that you yourself stumbled into such a hiding place.

"The levies couldn't risk carrying too many items at once – that would attract attention. No, they'd have to do it piecemeal, returning from their hiding place, after dark, to do so. That would also explain the strange shadows, noises, and 'moved objects' that the sappers reported.

"From your account, they took one of the little goat-tracks up into the hills, clearing their footprints, along with any other tracks, as they went – which is why Henn found none. They knew the territory. Knew the caves and hidden tunnels. Perhaps Henn even stood on top of one such tunnel, when one of the levies, hiding out below, made his rather ominous statement.

"As to what killed them? I believe I have a theory. Have you ever heard of 'wind of ball'?"

"Can't say I have."

"For as long as we've made war with black powder, there have been reports of men dying without any external injuries on their bodies. Sir Thomas Longmore devoted several pages to the phenomena in his rather interesting treatise on gunshot wounds. He described victims who had died without any marks of violence on their skin beyond symptoms of cerebral concussion. Despite this, their internal organs had become what he called 'viscus'.

"During the Napoleonic Wars, such deaths were observed by combatants on both sides. The same was reported during the American Civil War. It was long thought that the concussive power of the 'wind' created by the cannonball itself was the cause."

"So that's why Brennan remarked that there hadn't been any artillery practice!"

"Certainly. Did Brennan have family in the navy?"

"He did. But that still doesn't explain how the levies died."

"No, but I personally believe that Doctor Forbes, who was writing at the start of the century, had the truth of it. He suggested that the cause of such strange deaths wasn't a wind, but a *vacuum*, following in the wake of the cannonball. This would cause a sudden expansion and rupture of the fluids in the stomach, along with the blood in the blood vessels. The wind you mention, traveling low, and fast, trapped in a narrow pass, unable to escape the vertical cliffs, might create such a vacuum. Certainly, the epicenter of your dust-devil could."

"So that's it!" I cried, feeling, as I often did, foolish not to have seen the clues so clearly laid out before me.

"I believe so. Sadly, such a proposition leaves little room for *djinn*, I'm afraid."

"That's shame! I was rather hoping you might conjure up proof of a genie or two. Brennan and Henn would have enjoyed that."

"I assume . . . ?"

I shook my head. Brennan, Henn, and little Jimmy Johnson hadn't been as lucky as I.

"Well, then," Holmes said, raising his glass, "may I suggest a toast?"

"Of course."

"To absent – and present – friends."

"Here, here!"

Outside the window, I could see the fireman, stroking his chin, fresh snow falling into the hole he'd just cleared.

Once again my mind returned to Maiwand. To the wound I'd received there, which had put paid to my army career, and sent me, broken, back to England. It was a day which, for the longest time, I'd wished to forget, but which I now realized, had led me to London, to Baker Street, and to my Mary.

"Pass the port," I said to my dear friend and colleague. "It looks like it's going to be a long night. It wouldn't do to get a chill!"

NOTES

• Paddington Station was the London terminus of the Great Western Railway (GWR). Designed by Brunel, its glazed roof is supported by wrought-iron arches in three spans. The GWR first experimented with electric lighting in 1880, with Paddington Station being lit for Christmas that year. By 1886, the station was completely illuminated by electric light.

• The City and South London Railway began running trains on an electrified fourth rail in 1890. The route now forms part of the London Underground's Northern Line.

• The Express service that Watson refers to is likely The Cornishman, which began running between Paddington and Penzance, Cornwall, in 1890. The down train left Paddington at 10:15, and arrived at Plymouth at 13:50, making it the fastest west-coast service of the period. Today's travel times are little different.

• The Great Blizzard of 1891 was the worst storm Britain had experienced in generations. Snow and hurricane-force winds derailed trains, sank ships, and brought the country to a halt. One train was derailed and buried in snow, only to be discovered thirty-six hours later, by a farmer looking for lost sheep.

• The Battle of Maiwand took place on 27 July, 1880. Named for the nearby village in Afghanistan, the battle was part of the wider Second Anglo-Afghan War, with the British campaigning to stop Russian influence in Afghanistan, which threatened British India and the vital trade route through the Khyber Pass.

• Ali Musjid Fort was captured by the British after the Battle of Ali Masjid, on 21 November, 1878.

- The make-up of British forces in this period reflects the complexity of the political situation in the region. Some native forces, such as the Sikhs, allied themselves with the British, as they believed it was the best way to keep their independence from India. Other forces felt threatened by Russian-backed Afghanistan.
- James H. Johnson was one of five drummers listed as casualties at the Battle of Maiwand. Although boy drummers were romanticized in fiction, they were often adult men. Fourteen year-olds could enlist with their family's consent – but in poorer families, boys did lie about their age to join the army. James enlisted in 1875. If he joined when he was fourteen, he would have been seventeen or eighteen at this point. Watson's description implies that he appears younger, which may have been the result of the privations of army life on a child.
- Ali Musjid Fort was named for Alī ibn Abī Ṭālib, the cousin of the Prophet Muhammad. There is indeed a shrine there, and the region is considered holy.
- Genie, djinn, or jinn, have long been a feature of pre-Islamic folklore.
- Lieutenant Thomas Rice Henn, Royal Engineers, and Corporal Michael Brennan (66th Regiment, 2nd Battalion Berkshires), were both killed at Maiwand. During the battle, British forces were outnumbered ten-to-one and massively outgunned. It's reported that British ranks stood firm, their rifle barrels becoming so hot they had to wrap cartridge paper around their fingers to stop blistering.
- Despite almost a thousand men from Watson's regiment falling in battle, eleven made such a brave stand, covering their retreating comrades, that the Afghans reported their sacrifice with great respect. Lieutenant Henn and a handful of his sappers, supported by

native grenadiers, were amongst those eleven. They held the enemy at bay, fighting back-to-back until their ammunition was exhausted, before charging with bayonets. Every man was killed. In British military history, the action is known as "The Stand of the Last Eleven". The events are dramatized in Rudyard Kipling's poem "That Day". It was at Maiwand that Watson, positioned near the front, took a bullet which almost cost his life.

• Watson seems to have been ahead of the game here. Sir Garnet Wolseley, who in 1862 had been an observer of the American Civil War, had seen railway workers using cinder goggles. When, in 1882, he was made Adjutant-General to the Forces in Egypt, he encouraged his troops to use cinder goggles to keep dust and sand out of their eyes.

• Bobbie was the regimental mascot dog. The mongrel, from Reading, was owned by Sergeant Kelly. Bobbie survived the final stand of the Eleven and escaped, wounded, to join the retreat to Kandahar. On his return to England, he was presented with the Afghan War Campaign Medal by Her Majesty Queen Victoria at Osborne House.

• The Hazara are a Shia Muslim minority who have long been the subject of persecution in the region. Between 1888 and 1893, over sixty-percent the Hazara population were slaughtered by the Afghan Army.

• "Put the willies up me". The origin of the phrase is said to come from the 1840's ballet Giselle, where the spirits of wronged lovers are led by the Queen of the Wilis to exact their vengeance.

• The book Holmes mentions is Sir Thomas Longmore's A Treatise on Gunshot Wounds, published in 1862. Longmore was Deputy Inspector-General of Hospitals and Professor of Military

Surgery at Chatham. "Wind of ball" is also called wind of the shot, vent de boulet, and wind contusions.

• Doctor P. Forbes, writing in The Edinburgh Medical Journal of 1812, proposed that a vacuum, created by the passage of the cannonball, would suck air from the body and cause a sudden expansion of fluids in the body, rupturing organs and blood vessels.

• It's likely that Holmes is right and that the deaths were caused, not by the wind, but by the vacuum the wind created. The phenomena has been noted in the modern day Khyber Pass by locals and travelers. It is notable for what's described as winds that reach an ear-splitting crescendo. The swirling sand then creates a low pressure area a couple-of-hundred meters above the surface which, in turn, creates a vacuum.

The Case of the Bryniau Witch Tower

Holmes wandered around our rooms with his chin upon his chest, packing and repacking his pipe, with an attitude of weary forbearance. Eventually, pipe still unlit, he threw himself into his armchair and began thumbing through the morning papers.

He hummed tunelessly as he read, clearly finding nothing of interest in either the daily news or *The Police Gazette*. "It's no use," he finally said. "London has become too weary for words. One day I will write a monograph on the correlation between crime and temperature, for it's clear that as soon as the mercury rises, the criminal classes become absolute fools. There isn't a single crime, intrigue, or rumor here that a pudding-head like Lestrade couldn't muddle his way through."

"It *is* unseasonably hot for July," I ventured.

"What it is, is damnably dull! Honestly, Watson, if things don't improve, we may have to go on holiday, or something equally horrible," he replied theatrically.

"Sadly, the state of my finances means I'll be staying in London for the whole season." I sighed. I'd been itching to escape the smog and noise of the city for weeks, but voicing my predicament sent me into quite the funk.

"Oh, my dear fellow!" Holmes exclaimed, sounding contrite. "You should have said something. Come!" he cried, jumping up with one of his characteristic bursts of energy. "My own finances are healthy enough for two. Choose somewhere, and we'll be off this very morning."

I suspected that Holmes's idea of paradise was to spend the entire summer, blinds half-drawn, pipe wedged between his lips, so I was reluctant to let such an unexpected offer pass by.

I had just read an advertisement in *The Morning Chronicle* for a delightful-sounding place on the Welsh coast. So it was that, within the hour, we were headed to Euston and, from there to Llandudno – which the marketing men had nicknamed *"The Queen of Welsh Watering Places"*.

Our journey was so peaceful that I soon drifted into a sound sleep. One moment I was watching the sun rising over the patchwork of towns and factories that littered the English countryside, and the next, it seemed, our train was steaming along the coast, where sand and the fretful waves of the Irish Sea, unfolded before us.

Llandudno is named for Saint Tudno, one of the seven sons of Seithenyn, whose failure to maintain the sea defenses led to the drowning of his kingdom. In an attempt to atone for the sins of his father, Tudno established a small church on a huge limestone outcrop, known as the Great Orme's Head. A thousand years later, modern engineering has paved and terraced Tudno's massive rock, but it still dominates the town.

Indeed, we saw the Great Orme long before Llandudno itself came into view.

The tourists who flock to this picturesque resort will tell you that the name, *Great Orme*, comes from the Norse meaning *Great Wrym*, and there was something distinctly dragonish in its appearance. It loomed large over the town, its 'head' the most prominent feature, with its body curling around the peninsula. Wrapped as it was in a heavy mist, the effect was quite striking.

By the time our train had pulled into the station, I was eager to see what other delights our destination had to offer. I had been yearning to feel the wind in my hair, hear the crunch of shingle under my boots. So it was with a spring in my step that I alighted into the smoke-filled station.

The striking structure was perhaps four or five years old, and looked determinedly modern when compared to the smaller, provincial stations we'd seen en route. Red Ruabon bricks and finialed iron columns supported a vast glass canopy, which trapped both heat and steam within, creating a veritable Turkish bath.

The station's five platforms were filled with trains arriving and departing, and between them rushed an assortment of travelers and holiday-makers, all dressed for the summer, with their cares packed neatly away.

Between Platforms Two and Three ran a cobbled road, designed to allow hansoms to line up alongside the carriages, and it was there that we quickly found a cab.

We hadn't had time to make plans, or even pick a hotel, but after consulting the driver, we determined that The King's Head Public House would suit us very nicely, being on the edge of town, and close to the headland that the advertisement had made so much capital of.

"I have a suspicion," Holmes remarked to the ruddy-faced driver, "that my companion would rather walk. If you could deliver our luggage to the inn and secure us two rooms, we'd be very much obliged. But for now, where is this famous Great Orme that my friend is so keen to view?"

"Are you sure?" I asked Holmes, knowing that he neither shared my appreciation for nature, nor unwarranted exercise.

"My dear fellow," he replied, "based on the way you've been prowling around Baker Street, I'm fairly certain that should you spend another moment indoors – even if said indoors should prove to be deliciously cool and well-sprung – you're likely to explode. Besides, train carriages tend not to be designed for those with long limbs, and I could do with unknotting my legs."

"Well, it's a lovely day, mind," the driver intoned in a wonderfully sing-song accent. "As for *Y Gogarth*," he said, using what I assumed was the Welsh name for the hill, "you can't miss it." He gestured up and west, where the looming shadow of the Great Orme was perfectly visible through the station's glass canopy. "Take any road. They all lead up, eventually. It's quite a gentle walk, with plenty of places to stop and admire the view."

The man's instructions proved to be exact, and soon we were ascending the Orme with the sun on our faces, and a sea-breeze in our nostrils.

Before long, however, I was breathing hard and leaning into my cane. "Good Heavens!" I panted regarding the ever steepening road ahead with alarm. "I've climbed mountain passes in Peshawar that were less arduous than this!"

"Gentle indeed!" my companion laughed. "I'm beginning to suspect that Welshmen are part goat."

We ploughed on, feeling great sympathy for the poor pack animals we passed, who had been pressed into service hauling necessaries up and down the hill.

After thirty minutes of stumbling over a pathway rutted with the grooves of carriage wheels and the imprint of hobnails, we suddenly came to a row of stone cottages. And there, standing in the little garden, watering a row of potted plants, was Peter Jones, formerly of Scotland Yard.

It had been over six years since we'd encountered Inspector Jones, and at a glance, he seemed little changed. On closer inspection, he appeared leaner and fitter than the man who had been with us on that long vigil to apprehend John Clay in the bowls of the City and Suburban Bank.

He greeted us warmly, with a brisk handshake and a smile of delight.

"Well, as I live and breathe, if it isn't Mr. Holmes and Doctor Watson!"

"Country living suits you, Jones!" I exclaimed, genuinely pleased to see our old sparring-partner looking so well.

"They do say that!" the old police dog chuckled before waving us inside, where we found the little house delightfully compact and homey.

Jones invited us to sit while a woman, who he introduced as his sister, busied around, offering us tea and a type of flat scone made with currents, called a "Welsh cake".

Encouraged by Jones, I piled my plate high, and followed his example in liberally spreading the cakes with jam and butter. Thus provided with a much-needed – albeit much-delayed – breakfast, we settled down to get our breath.

"You retired then, Jones?" I asked.

"In a manner of speaking. After thirty years at the Yard, I had the chance to collect a pension which was equal to thirty-fiftieths of the pay. My baby sister, Nerys, had not long since lost her husband, and there was an opening for an inspector here. Well, I was starting to feel a little long in the tooth for chasing villains, and thirty-fiftieths pay is a little tight to live on in London, so it seemed a fine time to move back."

We made small talk for long enough for my legs to forget the steepness of the hill, then headed back out to attempt the summit.

"Very obliged for the refreshments, Jones," Holmes said, as we waved our farewells, "and should you need anything at all, we'll be staying in The King's Head."

My friend had once called Jones "an absolute imbecile". I prided myself on not being quite such an idiot.

"So, how long have you known that Jones was in Wales?" I asked, finding it hard to feel as annoyed as I should, with such spectacular views unfolding before us.

My friend gave me a sheepish grin. "Since last year, but remember: It was your choice to come here . . . ."

I shot him my best disapproving look. "And I suppose it was pure coincidence that I happened upon *The Morning Chronicle* and its pages – creased just so – fell open at a quarter-page advertisement for Inspector Jones's new beat?"

Holmes gave a small, embarrassed cough. "Sorry. Guilty as charged. But come, now, my dear Watson. You would have manfully gone through the whole summer without a break had I not determined that Llandudno could offer us both a much-needed respite. What is it Monsieur Taine says? *'We travel to change, not to change a place, but to change ideas.'*"

I wasn't about to let him off the hook. "And I suppose your spiderish networks told you exactly where the inspector could be found? Although knowing he would be watering his plants exactly as we walked past is a remarkable piece of prestidigitation, even for you!"

"There is such a thing as co-incidence, you know," Holmes replied, sounding abashed. "Although, had we not been so lucky, I imagine I'd have been compelled to knock for a glass of water . . . ."

"Well, don't think I'm going to forgive you so easily!"

He looked so shamefaced that I couldn't help but smile and soon, we were both chuckling heartily. It wasn't until we had climbed over the headland, that the beauty of the scene stopped all further laughter.

The sun was high now and there, before us, lay the sparkling sea. Small sail boats bobbed up and down on the horizon while, overhead, curlew called mournfully to their mates.

I did not know what the scientific explanation was for the curious way the rays of sun broke through the clouds, like spotlights illuminating the land below, but in that moment, I fancied that Wales itself was telling me "*Here. You may take your rest here.*"

And rest I did.

Late afternoon had turned to early evening by the time we left the soft heather and scent of wild flowers behind, to begin our descent.

Soon, we were back on the same dust track we had ascended and before us, once again, lay the little row of miner's cottages where we had met Jones.

Suddenly Holmes let out a low cry. "Ho! What's this?"

It was some time before I spotted what Holmes's eagle-eyes had seen. There, silhouetted in the doorway of his cottage, stood Jones and a uniformed officer, deep in conversation.

The young constable gave a little start as we approached. I saw his face, pale and serious, and something in his attitude made my heart sink.

Holmes lengthened his stride, and it wasn't long before he had joined the conclave. As for myself, my knees protested horribly at the steepness of the track, and by the time I had caught up, it was clear that Holmes had already learned the reason for the solemn expressions and hushed tones.

"It's bad, Watson," he said, in a voice heavy with tension. He looked at Jones, who turned to give me the full weight of his regard.

"Mr. Holmes has already explained that you're in sore need of a sabbatical, but if you can help, it's a doctor we need now."

"You surely have doctors on call?" Holmes sounded so defensive that I instantly forgave him his previous machinations.

"This is a holiday town. On a warm weekend like this, every doctor is run off his feet setting bones and treating sunstroke. And none of them – not even the coroner – is *Doctor Watson*." He gave such weight to those final words that I felt myself blush.

"I really am so sorry, my dear fellow," Holmes said.

"Nonsense. Jones, Constable, I'm entirely at your disposal. If the fates have put us here, then let us do what we can."

There's nothing more wretched than a young woman in the full flush of life who has made that final climb up the golden staircase. As a doctor. I knew death in all its forms. Many times, it comes as a blessed release. For others, it's a painless journey. This young lady's death was neither of those things.

Enfys Tegwen was a lively, popular girl. She worked as a shop assistant, sang in the chapel choir, and sent money home to her elderly father in Bala every week.

Enfys lodged with two other girls in an attic room above Arthur's General Store, where all three worked.

That Saturday, she had asked for a day's leave to visit her sick father. The girl had no other relatives, so the store's owner readily agreed. She was away all day, and all night.

Saturday closing wasn't until half-past-eight, and Enfys's co-workers didn't get home until nine. When they rose the next morning for chapel, she still hadn't returned, which surprised them as she was diligent about attending. After chapel, the girls walked on the promenade, then along the pier, stretching out those little pleasantries as long as possible, as people do when they have the luxury of a free day, without any spare money to spend.

They returned to their lodgings around three, which is when they found their friend's body, curled up on her bed, dead.

She'd been sick – violently so, several times. Her dress and the bedsheets were bloodied and, from the position of her body, it was clear that she had suffered violent convulsions in the moments leading up to her death.

She was so pale, and there was so much blood, that it was clear she'd bled to death in this sad, little garret. But what had caused her to bleed in such a dramatic fashion? That was the question that occupied me.

I already had my suspicions, but a glass and an empty tin on the bedside table confirmed them. Inside both was the residue of a white powder – and it was this which revealed the lady's tragic story.

I handed it to Jones. "Hmm, sweets?" he said, looking at the label. "But Pollards aren't Welsh. They're based in the Midlands – Leamington Spa. My old Da always swore by their toffee. Had to order it for him by mail. Not cheap." He peered into the tin, sniffing experimentally. "Well that's not toffee, that's for sure."

"I'll have to do some tests to be certain, but I've vouch its diachylon or similar."

"Lord!" the inspector whispered, clearly sensible of my meaning.

While I worked, Holmes prowled the room, looking for all those tiny details that would help piece together the poor girl's last moments.

"Mmm . . . we've been lucky. The black paint on the boards is relatively new. There's little scuffing beyond this patch, between the bed and the door. See here: The marks from two sets of shoes. One is a lady's walking boot, the other are a pair of men's lightweight dress shoes."

His face was almost pressed against the floorboards. Yet from his expression, it seemed that whatever patterns had revealed themselves to him, they were not as clear as he would have wished.

"The scuffs are confused, seeming to lead from the door to the bed, then back again. Was there a struggle? Was the lady dragged to the bed, and held down? Indentations on the mattress suggest that someone did indeed hold her down. You'll have noted the bruises around her wrists, Doctor, as well as the strands of red hair on the collar of her dress. Note that neither of her roommates are red-haired."

He paused, looking absorbed. "But what does this diachylon have to do with her death, Watson? It's it's a simple household medicament – No?"

As a student, I'd seen women admitted to Barts in desperate condition as the result of what was termed a "backstreet abortion". It happened more often than we men would like to admit, and not always to unmarried women. Such procedures were dangerous, but no more so than the purgatives and abortifacients advertised, quite publicly, for their ability to resolve "female irregularities".

"You're quite right. Ordinarily, diachylum is used to make plasters to treat cuts and sores. It's part of every housewife's medicine cabinet. However, as many women have discovered, *diachylum* is a preparation of white lead. In sufficiently large doses, it causes headaches, vomiting, and miscarriages."

If the lady had taken it willingly, then I would have reported this as a tragic accident. Exsanguination as the result of a miscarriage. The family need not be further distressed by the details. But Holmes had raised an interesting point: Did someone force Enfys to digest the contents of this tin? If so, he or she may not have intended her murder, but murder it was.

Notwithstanding their distress, the girls waiting outside the attic room proved to be sensible and thoughtful witnesses.

Jones quickly ascertained that Enfys had, as they termed it, been "visiting with a young gentleman" for at least four months. Neither girl knew his name, nor had seen him. She often stayed away overnight, too, implying some secret tryst.

Enfys herself had let slip scant clues as to the identity of her mystery caller. He was, according to Judy Meredith, "free with his money", for in the last month she'd seen Enfys in two new dresses, and wearing "a rainbow brooch".

"These dresses," Holmes asked, "would be the navy blue one and the yellow one, in her trunk?"

"That's right."

"And this brooch – there are pin marks on her dress, but it isn't here in the room. When did you last see her wearing it?"

"Why, she hasn't taken it off since she was gifted it," the doe-eyed girl called Nia replied, adding for clarification that, "Enfys means rainbow in Welsh."

"I see. Would one have to be a Welsh-speaker to know that?"

"I should think so, sir."

"And what else did you notice? Please, think carefully."

"A couple of times," Judy commented, "I caught her crying. I knew she was very keen on this gent, but she'd seen him walking out with some young widow, and she worried that she was too plain, too poor, and was sure to lose him."

"What sort of man would do that?" Jones said with a flush of tenderness that was surprising in such an old Scotland Yard bulldog. "Playing a pretty girl like that. Shameful!"

"What sort of a man? Hmm," Holmes replied, distractedly. "Let us see what we have so far, shall we? He's a liberal gift-giver. However, the dresses he bought are second or third-hand. You can see where they have been re-cut. His shoes were likely costly but have been much repaired – the imprint of patches are quite visible on the boards. So he's a man who wishes to impress, but has limited resources, or spends beyond his means.

"Shoe size generally is proportional to height, so he is at least six foot tall. He's a Welsh-speaker, has red-hair, and wears a signet ring on the middle finger of his right hand – the mark left by it can be seen on the poor girl's wrist. And the brooch – I wonder if the lady returned it, or was it taken? Regardless, it's surely unusual enough to trace."

"Ho!" Jones cried. "No need! We have him! There's only one man in town who fits that description: Granville Baughn!" He said it like a curse. "The family business is the sort of big, dirty industry we have in Wales: Mines, and quarries, and the like. They're hardworking people who've done well for themselves. Not as well as some, but they're respectable and ambitious. They place great hopes on Granville, who is their only child and, frankly, Mr. Holmes, a stain on their good name. He's a drinker, a gambler, a profligate. Spends freely, and not afraid to borrow when funds run low. He wants something, he takes it. That includes other men's wives and other men's sweethearts." There was something in the way that Jones weighted those last words that made me wonder if *he* had a wife or sweetheart.

"He's been arrested a score of times – nothing that stuck. I couldn't say if he has a good lawyer, or we have bad police, but he seems to have a charmed life. No matter how many drunken brawls, no matter how many accusations of fraud or theft, he's never held to account. But we have him here, Mr. Holmes. We have him here!"

"I'm not so sure," Holmes answered, quietly.

"Oh?"

"Just this: Diachylum is freely available from any pharmacy, yet it was sold or given to Granville in this tin. That suggests that the person who gave it to him was trying to disguise it as something else."

"But Enfys must have known what the tin contained," I said. "Why else would she struggle so?"

"If we assume that the lady wanted to keep the child, but Granville Baughn did not, then that's quite a sound assumption, Doctor. But what if we look at the evidence another way? The scuffs on the floor . . . Let us suppose they lead from the bed to the door. So the lady takes the powder, and falls ill. Granville may have been assisting her, rather than compelling her – trying to help her to a doctor, perhaps? She takes a turn for the worse, so he drags her back to the bed. The indentations on the mattress, the bruises around her wrists – she was convulsing. In that instance, would you not attempt to hold someone down to stop them from injuring themselves?"

"Are you suggesting that neither Granville nor Enfys knew what was in the tin?"

" Why else would you disguise its contents?"

"Why, indeed?"

"Look, Mr. Holmes, we have Granville bang to rights on this!" Jones interjected. "Why, the boy could have bought the diachylon himself, and put it in this tin to pretend it was some harmless thing."

"But the lady struggled!" I said.

"Did she now? Or maybe when he saw how sick she was, he tried for a doctor, as Mr. Holmes suggested." Jones nodded to the constable who had been diligently guarding the door to the attic room. "Williams, I want you to head over to the Imperial. Granville keeps rooms there. Grab a couple of extra constables on the way and bring him to the station. I'll be along shortly."

"Of course, it's your case, Inspector," Holmes commented, "but even if Granville is our man, there are still too many questions that need to be answered. Tell me, Watson: How widely known are the effects of diachylon?"

"Most married ladies would know of it. Would Granville? Unlikely. It's hardly spoken of in polite company."

"I see. By-the-by, Jones, who might single ladies, with no mothers to consult, go to for help with such things hereabouts?"

Jones is a big man but as Holmes spoke, he suddenly seemed to deflate. "Oh, Lord! Dinah Davis!"

"And who is Dinah Davis?" Holmes asked, his keen eyes shining.

"Only the local witch, Mr. Holmes. Only the bloomin' local witch! She lives in an old ruin, close to Thomas Barker's antimony mine."

"How interesting" Holmes murmured. "Did you know that antimony is used to harden lead?"

We were seated in a hansom heading towards a place Jones called the Bryniau Watch Tower – a seventeenth-century structure built to warn coastal communities of Barbary slavers. The area was made up of ancient smallholdings nestled amongst medieval ruins, lying just outside the town.

"So, Jones," Holmes said, his voice steady and sober, "tell me about witches."

"It's embarrassing, but the truth is that there's many in these parts who still take this sort of thing very seriously. You see, there's always been cunning folk in Wales that people go to with their problems."

"What sort of problems?"

"Oh, women's things, mainly."

"In the past," I said by way of explanation, "most communities would have a wise woman of some sort – skilled in herbalism, traditional medicine. Someone to deliver babies and such . . . ."

"That's right, Doctor. Only there's no 'in the past' about it. Wales has always been a bit more inclined towards the magical and the mystical. They burnt witches in England. In Wales, they gave them good silver and their thanks. Indeed, the Welsh like their cunning folk, and while we're a proudly Christian country, there's a barely town or village where you won't find one still plying their trade. Good folk, mostly, but some really do deserve the name witch!"

"You can't be serious?" I spluttered.

Holmes nodded thoughtfully. "Oh, I think, my dear Watson, you underestimate how hard it is to shake off beliefs that have been part of life for thousands of years. Why, I've recent accounts in my files of people being sent to the Assizes for hiring witches, of men and women accused of witchcraft – even murdered for it. As Jones says, many of these cunning folk are simply blessed with a little medical know-how. But others play on much older superstitions. Perhaps they even believe in it themselves."

"Witchcraft isn't on the statue books any longer?" I remarked, not at all sure that was actually the case.

"True, although it is illegal for persons to pretend or profess to tell fortunes, or to use any subtle craft, means, or device to deceive and impose. This Davis woman, Jones: Does she claim to be a witch?"

"Not openly, but it's known that she's the person to go to for charms, potions, and the like."

"There's a great deal of difference between making herbal remedies and deliberately causing hurt." Holmes said, quietly. "Which is it? After all, not everyone can afford a doctor. As for love potions – Well, if the price of hope is a ha'penny concoction, what harm is there in that?"

"I agree and, until today, I've had no reason to believe Davis is anything other than an inoffensive old woman, trading rose-water charms for gin money."

"And women's problems?"

"Let's just say that no one has gone out of their way to draw my attention to such things. And I haven't gone out of my way to look into it. But if you're right, and Davis did supply Enfys with the powder, well . . . the law is the law."

"Do you intend to arrest her?" I asked.

In lieu of an answer, Jones rapped on the cab's roof, as a signal for the driver to stop.

In London, our night skies are so clouded in smoke that one can rarely see the stars. In this corner of Wales, however, the sky was bright, and the gleaming stars cast a golden glow over the hillside.

We were only a few miles from the garish jollity of the holiday town, but the land felt positively primitive. Bats and owls flapped overhead, mice and voles skittered across our feet, and the eyes of animals – wild and domestic – shone at us out of the gloom.

Jones warned us to watch our feet, as once we were off the road, the "going would get tricky" – and so it was.

A rabbit hole brought me down, hard. Jones himself stumbled and swore as he fought to untangle his legs from the brambles and wild gorse. A wind rose, howling in our ears, tugging at our hair, and with it came a chill that felt like the icy fingers of some ancient Celtic spirit, angry at being disturbed.

Nature fought us, and every step we took seemed a struggle. Had I been a superstitious man, I might have looked up at the watch tower and shuddered to think on the witch who lived there who, even now, was listening to our approach.

Only Holmes – as sure-footed as ever – seemed immune to the curious atmosphere of the place. He set his aquiline features to the wind and ploughed on, clambering over the piles of tumbled-down rocks with enviable ease.

We were close enough now to see the old ruin – and how cunningly it had been re-purposed.

It was a round, rubble-stone affair, about twenty foot in height and perhaps the same in internal diameter. The northeast wall was missing, but a hovel built of drystone had been set against it.

A roof constructed of timber and a simple bramble thatch covered the whole. The lower levels had been smeared with pitch, presumably to proof it against the elements. The upper stage of the tower revealed a window, covered in some kind of sail cloth, and in it was set a storm lantern, its bright orange flame busily bobbing against the elements.

Dinah Davis had clearly heard us coming. She met us at the door of the hovel, where she stood, buffeted by the wind, tying a tall black hat over a shock of dark, unruly curls.

Dressed in the traditional Welsh costume of hat, petticoat-like skirt, and woolen cloak, she looked like a picture-book witch come to life.

She could have been anywhere between forty to fifty years old, yet her face was so pinched, and her skin so sallow, that she looked much older.

She regarded us with large, dark eyes, arms folded defensively across her chest. Her greeting was warm enough, but her smile made it no further than her mouth, which was pursed and thin.

The front of the hovel was so low that all three of us had to bend to enter. It was a sorry sort of dwelling. A pair of chairs and table were set beside the door. Further in, against the tower's far wall, was a tiny bed, another chair, and a pair of old sea chests.

Makeshift wooden shelves virtually filled the wall of the tower, where books fought for space with rows and rows of old sweet jars and tins. Labels were attached to each one describing the contents in a neat, cursive script.

"We've come to speak to you about Enfys Tegwen," Jones said.

"Then speak," Davis replied.

"May we?" the inspector gestured to the tower end of the house. "It would be more comfortable for us all if we could sit."

"Do as you will." The lady took off her hat and headed for the little bed, where she positioned herself, while Holmes and I carried the chairs through.

Thus seated, Jones began.

"We've reason to believe that you were recently visited by Enfys Tegwen and Granville Baughn. Can you tell us why they came to see you?"

"No secret to it. Baughn had ruined another young girl and expected me to help him keep his good name."

"And did you?"

"I did nothing for him."

"Don't lie to me now, Dinah!"

"Pssh!" the old lady hissed, clearly irritated. "Don't you 'Dinah' me! It's 'Miss Davis' to you, and I may be many things, but I'm no liar. You can ask Enfys yourself."

Jones took a deep breath. "I'm afraid that Miss Tegwen isn't in a position to speak to anyone anymore."

I saw Davis give a little start. For a moment I thought the news had rendered her speechless. Then she suddenly exploded into a paroxysm of rage.

Dinah Davis was barely five foot tall, and as thin as a switch, but in that moment she seemed to fill the room.

She leapt to her feet. The light from the flickering lanterns, set on either side of the tower, cast elongated shadows on the walls, so that it seemed there was an ever growing army of old ladies. They bobbed and whirled around the room, and in the centre of the maelstrom stood Dinah Davis, her back ramrod straight, fists clenched, her unblinking eyes aflame.

"No, no, no! Say it isn't true! Say it isn't true?" She repeated the same phrases several times, her tiny frame shaking so much that I feared she would give herself an apoplexy.

"My dear Miss Davis," Holmes said, in that gentle way he has, "please, sit. Calm yourself."

Davis looked at Holmes as though she was searching for something in his cool, grey eyes. I do not know what she found, but she held his gaze for longer than I would have found comfortable. As she did so, her breathing slowed, and the color began to return to her face.

"We're sorry to be the bringer of bad news," Holmes began. "You mentioned that he had 'ruined another girl'. Had he been to see you before?"

"No. But most girls in trouble will go their mother, or an older, married friend, but poor Enfys had no one."

"Tell us," Holmes said, his eyes still fixed on Davis, his face a mask.

The old witch smoothed her skirts, pulled her cloak around her shoulders, and began:

"This was Saturday, just after ten in the morning. I'd never seen either of them before, but I knew Granville. Knew the sort of man he was. All charm and talk – He will tell a girl what she wants to hear. Anything she's foolish enough to believe. Oh, how they coddle and cajole, these little princes. *Rich in will, weak in willpower*' These *liars! Deceivers! Palterers!*"

As she spoke, her voice rose, and her eyes took on a faraway look.

In the closeness of that ancient tower, her words echoed strangely and their rhythm had a curious effect on me. I recalled reading Tacitus's account of Rome's Legions arriving on the Isle of Anglesey, only to find themselves facing an army of wild-haired Druids, throwing curses into the wind. Davis had something of that. An attitude both primitive and knowing. I felt the hair on the back of my neck prickle and a shudder came, unbidden.

For a moment, it seemed that Davis was lost to us in some Druidic past. Then, with a blink of those huge eyes, she was back.

The lady herself didn't seem to know that her mind had wandered, and resumed her account, quite unaware of the curious impact it had had on her listeners.

"He put on a good show, I'll say for him. Lots of talk about 'being too young to start a family yet' and 'wanting to do right by his intended'. I didn't believe a word of it.

"I asked him to leave us so that we women could speak freely. She told me, straight – Granville had persuaded her to come, but she wanted to keep the baby. I can see her now: Pitiful child, so trusting. 'He wants to do things right' she said. 'He's says we'll have plenty of time for a family later, but his parents will think badly of me if I go to the altar pregnant.'"

"So Granville had made her an offer of marriage?"

"That's what she believed."

Holmes fished around in the voluminous pockets of his sack coat and produced the Pollard's tin. He asked Davis to look inside it.

"Have you ever," he asked, "given anyone such a substance?"

"If a lady is out of order, and not too far along, then hellebore, savin, tansy, or pennyroyal will restore the courses. That's what I would recommend. *Recommend*, mind," she added, looking pointedly at Jones.

"So you gave her nothing?"

"I didn't say that. I gave her a powder to help with the baby – and instructions on how to take it."

"A restorative?" I asked.

"Exactly that."

"Tell me, Miss Davis: How did Baughn react when you told him Miss Tegwen wanted to keep the child. Was he angry?" Jones asked the question, but I could see Holmes's eyes, fixed on Davis.

"He said they would go home and talk some more. That he would abide by her decision. But I was afraid for the girl."

"You thought he would harm her?" Holmes queried.

"I didn't say so."

"No, Miss Davis, I notice that you're very careful about what you say. So I'll repeat the question: Did you think that Mr. Baughn posed a danger to Miss Tegwen?"

Miss Davis didn't reply immediately. Instead, she wrapped her hands around herself in a curious manner, appearing, once again, to be elsewhere. Then, as before, she blinked those remarkable eyes, and seemed to remember herself. "I think," she said, in a voice that was brittle and hard, "that people like Mr. Baughn always pose a danger to people like Miss Tegwen."

With that, the interview was at an end and we were ejected back onto the hillside wherein lay the bones of the long dead.

"Well, that's that" Jones commented, as we trudged back down the slope towards the waiting cab. "It looks like Baughn's our man."

"Oh, indeed?" Holmes sniffed. "You don't find anything strange about Miss Davis's statement?"

"She's a strange women, to be sure, and there may be a case to answer about her wider activities. But it's clear to me that Baughn didn't want this child and, having failed to procure what he needed from Davis, likely consulted with one of his other women about how to deal with it. Maybe that rich widow of his? We'll know more once we get to the station."

"Clear? No it isn't clear, Inspector. Nothing is clear, apart from the fact that Dinah Davis might be 'many things, but not a liar'. Isn't that what she said?"

"Exactly!" Jones huffed. "She told us the truth."

"No. She didn't lie. There's a difference."

"Now look here, Mr. Holmes, you have your methods. They're a little too theoretical and fantastical for me, but you've always been a great help to the police, so if you've something on your mind that has a bearing on this case, then out with it."

Holmes answered Jones's question answered with another: "What do you know of her? This supposed witch? What's her history?"

"Lord knows! Some say she's an educated woman. Worked in one the fashionable Midland towns as a governess. Fell on hard times, and came home to Wales. That's the story."

"Well," Holmes observed, "she writes with an educated hand and has an interesting library for a women in such dire straits,"

"Indeed," I added. "Not many living as she does could quote Shakespeare."

"Ah, thank you, Doctor!" Holmes replied. "There seemed something familiar about *'rich in will'*, but it's a very long time since I studied the Bard."

Back in the hansom, Holmes sank back in his seat, consumed by his thoughts – and I was left alone with mine. So dark were they that I was pleased, once again, to see the lights of the seaside town and hear the cheery voices of the holidaymakers as they passed by, taking in the night air.

I still couldn't shake off the image of Dinah Davis, railing to the gods about Granville Baughn. Or was it Baughn that she referenced? At that moment, I looked at Holmes, and I knew that he, too, had come to the same realization. And, for the second time since we had become embroiled in this case, my heart sank.

Granville Baughn lay on the slab on the little parish mortuary. It felt strange to finally see someone who had been spoken of so freely, and with such ill will, but here he was.

He had a shock of shoulder-length red hair, a pale face, and looked so painfully young that it took my breath away to see him. I was reminded immediately of Wallis's painting of

The Death of Chatterton – the romantic poet who had poisoned himself with arsenic in a fit of despair.

Baughn had been found by the constables who had been sent to detain him, his throat slashed by the cut-throat razor which was discovered beside him. He had left no note, and the door-man spoke of him arriving at the Imperial in a state of such distress that he'd ignored the familiar greetings of the hotel's other long-term residents.

He had been dead long enough for *rigor* to have set in. "That puts the time of death not long after Enfys's," I noted.

It was with some difficulty that we prized open the clenched fist that lay on his chest, over his heart. It contained the golden rainbow brooch that he had given to Enfys. It was such a sad sight that I felt tears come, unbidden, and was forced to step away to collect myself.

"Have you read William James, Watson?" Holmes uttered *sotto voce*, sounding much as I felt. "Interesting fellow. American. He wrote about how ideas, feelings, and sensations, both present and past, cohere into the experience of what he calls 'a continuous self'. For Dinah Davis, the past – her past – is ever present, and when she saw Enfys, she saw herself. You noticed the way she talked, how she cradled *something* – something small, something needing her protection. And how none of that seemed to have anything to do with Granville or Enfys.

"This lady has been poorly used – so poorly used that she fled from her life to hide away, here, in Wales. I imagine, Inspector, that should we look for traces of Dinah Davis in Leamington Spa, we would fill in the gaps of this tragic tale. Jones – you did say that she'd lived in the Midlands? I wonder what happened to her baby? The baby that ruined her life."

"And made her determined that no other young girl should have to endure the shame of being an unmarried mother?"

"That's exactly it, Watson. What was it she called the powder that she gave to Miss Tegwen? A *'restorative –* ' something to restore health and well-being. Which, to her, meant restoring Enfys to her previous condition. I believe she had no ill-intent. She simply couldn't believe in Granville. She'd been too injured by her own past."

Jones had sent constables to arrest Davis as soon as he had heard the news about Granville. He now stood, coat lapels turned up, hands deep in his pockets, puffing out little plumes of chill mortuary air. "Lord, but this is a mess!" he repeated, for the sixth time since we'd arrived.

"Dinah told us that Granville and Enfys intended to go home and talk. We must assume that he did, indeed, decide to abide by her decision to keep the child. He must have encouraged her to drink the powder – thinking it a tonic for the baby. Imagine his horror. His terror. His guilt! He couldn't have known what would happen should he have gotten the dose of the 'tonic' even slightly wrong. And what of Davis? The most

I can charge her with is supplying poison with intent to procure a miscarriage. Should I do that, then every desperate woman will pushed to take even more desperate actions. I'm loathe to do it, but the law *is* the law."

"I think Dinah Davis would be far better in a medical institute than a criminal one," I sniffed, suddenly feeling very tired.

Jones nodded. "You may be right at that, Doctor."

It had been almost ten hours since we'd arrived in this beautiful holiday resort. Our bags still lay, unclaimed, in The King's Head, our beds unused. "There are times when what one needs most in the whole world is a pipe, a brandy, and some convivial company," I mused, to no one in particular.

Jones looked first to myself and then to Holmes. "Sorry to say that Wales is dry on Sundays," he replied. "But I do have a pack of Grousemoor tobacco, a bottle of fine brandy, and a garden with the best views in the whole of Llandudno, should you consider an old Scotland Yard dullard like myself convivial enough."

I looked at Holmes and Jones, suddenly feeling a rush of affection for all those times that Baker Street had been my bulwark against the world. No matter how dire, no matter how tragic the events that overtook us, I knew I could always rely on the warmth of the companionship I found there.

Holmes was right. Sometimes you needed a change of place to change your perspective.

"I think, Inspector," I replied, smiling, "that might be exactly what the Doctor ordered."

NOTES

• Saint Tudno is the patron saint of Llandudno. He founded the original parish church on the Great Orme in the Sixth Century. The present twelfth-century church stands on the same site.

• Watson is quite right. The "modern" station, parts of which still stand, was built in 1892, replacing a much older structure.

• Etruria Marl clay is found in the Ruabon area of Wales. Its discovery heralded the beginning of mass tile and terracotta production. So-called Ruabon bricks get their rich red color from the clay's high iron content.

• The King's Head, named after King William IV (1765-1837), is the only pub surviving from old Llandudno before the development of the modern resort.

• Hippolyte Taine (1828-1893) was a French historian, critic, and philosopher.

• London police were one of the earliest professions to have a pension. Police paid a premium out of their own wages, in the hope that it would induce men to join and remain in the service, which was a poorly paid profession.

• Leamington Spa water is a mild laxative. Spa water toffees were taken for a similar effect.

• For most of history, abortion has been commonplace. Even amongst the early Puritan settlers to America, *abortifacients* were so widely known and used that Benjamin Franklin included a well-known recipe for one in his book, *The American Instructor, Or, Young Man's Best Companion* from 1759. In 1803, the first specific British law to deal with abortion made it punishable by the death penalty. The 1861 law removed the death penalty, but made administering drugs or using instruments to procure abortion punishable by life in prison. Despite this, many products were sold under the promise of *"restoring female regularity"*, *"removing obstructions"*, and dealing with *"delayed periods"*. One 1897 advertisement for Beechams's Powders appeared in the *Christian Herald* with the motto: *"Worth a guinea a box . . . for all bilious and nervous disorders . . . and female ailments."*

• When a water source became polluted by lead, causing a spate of miscarriages, diachylon, which was known to contain white lead, became a popular choice. Such products, as well as backstreet abortions, remained a fact of life for working class women until abortion was legalized in 1967. These highly dangerous products and procedures killed many thousands of women who, like poor Enfys, bled to death, or died of infections. Others were left infertile. Diachylon had the added danger of lead poisoning if it was used too often.

• In England and Scotland, around five-thousand women were sentenced to death for witchcraft. Only five witches were executed in Wales, where "cunning folk" were indeed largely well-regarded unless they caused harm. Those who were killed appeared to have fallen foul of the powerful and the wealthy.

• Barbary pirates terrorized coastal communities in the Mediterranean, Britain, and Ireland for almost two-hundred-and-fifty years, beginning in the seventeenth century. The Bryniau Watch Tower is believed to be the remains of a tower built to give coastal communities advance warning of pirate attacks. Its remains are still visible today. *Bryniau* means *"hill"* in Welsh. It's pronounced *"brin-y-I"* with a rolling *"R"*.

• The 1824 Vagrancy Act outlawed persons pretending or professing to be able to use magical powers. Accusations of witchcraft continued to appear in legal records throughout the 1850's and 1860's. The last witch trail in Britain happened in 1944.

- Psychologist William James coined the term "stream of thought" in 1890. His interest was in the "wandering mind", and how our internal stream of consciousness can be used to explore "the mind within"
- *"Rich in Will"* comes from Shakespeare's *Sonnet 135*.
- The battle Tacitus wrote of happened in 60 CE, between Druids on the Isle of Anglesey and the troops of General Suetonius Paulinus.

The author, who moved to Wales in 2023, can see the Bryniau Tower from the end of her street. This photo was taken during a walk given by the Great Orme Exploration Society (GOES), of which she is a member.

The Case of the Covent Garden Medium

We never talk about Mary.

I didn't know how much Holmes had gleaned about the circumstances surrounding my bereavement – nor had I asked. It was enough that he did know, and had shown his concern in those little ways that friends do. I understood that he would never press me for details – and I gave none, for while loss is something that every man must bear, how he bears it is for him, alone, to decide.

It may seem proof of some deep personal failing that the woman with whom I had shared so many wonderful years was an enigma to those closest to me. Outside of the social niceties, I rarely spoke of her. What we had seemed so precious that we felt no need to share it with the world. Together, we were complete.

The day that I had stood, peering down at the black rocks of Reichenbach Falls, listening to the dull echo of my own voice reverberating off the cliffs, I believed I would never again feel such emptiness. But that was as nothing compared to the loss of my Mary. My dear, sweet wife, Mary, who had made my life richer than I had ever hoped, and who had left me so suddenly, I felt I could not endure it.

I had held her hand, and breathed in her last breath as a kiss. I had draped our door handle with black crepe, and tied it with a ribbon. I had watched her small coffin being lowered into the earth. I had endured the million-and-one things society requires of the grieving husband, before returning to our empty home to endure the ticking of the clock, and the passage of the hours, alone.

For months, I had found myself setting the table for two, pulling up her chair near the fire every evening. I knew that it was mere grief, working its loathsome tricks upon me, but sometimes, as I sat reading in silence, I would have sworn that I'd heard the sound of her laugh, felt the brush of her fingers on my shoulder, as she walked past to take her seat in the easy-chair beside mine.

Then, without warning, the friend who had been lost to me was found. Inexplicably, extraordinarily, alive, and as vital and as real as I remembered. The joy of that moment was as a panacea to my grief, which was so new that I still wore my mourning weeds.

Now, our lives have returned to their old, familiar pattern at Baker Street and I find myself wondering: *What of Mary?* I'm not so far gone as to hope for the impossible, but I have good reason to wonder about the permanency of death.

Such thoughts had been my companion for some time, until the day I was approached with a proposition that threw my mind and spirit into turmoil.

"Calamity" Smith is my publisher at *The Strand* magazine. He's a tall, lean, no-nonsense chap, with a penchant for tobacco and word-puzzles. It was he who had been instrumental in putting Holmes's adventures before the wider public. Since then, we've met socially many times, and I've come to think of him as a friend.

Smith's usual lunch venue was The Albion. Close to both the British Museum's reading rooms and Fleet Street, it's usually packed with academics, actors, and authors. The air is Bohemian and unpretentious, with a quaint dining room partitioned into booths to afford privacy, and a smoking room which is one of the most pleasant of its kind in London.

One day, in late July of 1895, I determined that a stint at the Albion was exactly what I needed to shake off my funk. Holmes was busy and, in need of good food and convivial conversation, I'd called at Smith's offices, timing my arrival so that I might tempt him out to lunch.

The Strand is a delightful thoroughfare, whose eastern end is home to many of the nation's most popular publications. This includes *The Strand* magazine, which perversely stands in Southampton Street, in a handsome building with a triple entrance bounded by large plate-glass windows. One enters by the left door, where a spacious room, decorated in pale tints of salmon, green, and cream is given a more sober appearance by the addition of heavy mahogany doors and partitions. It's a building designed to impress, lined with bookshelves, and wired throughout for electric lights and telephones.

Smith's airy offices boast large windows overlooking the street, and even though padded chairs are provided for visitors, it's still very much a work room – and one piled with manuscripts and India-paper proofs.

The publisher is almost my age, with a pair of fine mustaches and a *pince-nez* that he balances on his nose in such a way that, when he looks directly at you, it gives one the impression of being thoroughly examined.

"Ah, Watson!" he said, as I entered, "just the man I wanted to see!"

Benjamin Franklin noted that time is money, and I've found that newspaper men take that aphorism very much to heart. Before I'd even had time to broach the topic of lunch, Smith had waved me to a chair and launched into a conversation which he declared" would be of great interest to both of us".

"What do you know of spiritualism?" he asked.

"Lord!" I said, stunned to be asked about a topic which had been so much in my thoughts. "Not a lot."

"*Do you believe?*" he queried, looking directly at me over his eyeglasses.

His question gave me pause. "I cannot say," I answered truthfully. "Oh, I'm sure that some of these people are in deadly earnest, but what I read of table-tilting and levitating seems like pure showmanship. Why, if the dead want to speak to us, I'm sure they could do so without ringing bells in shuttered rooms."

Smith nodded soberly. "*The Strand*, so far, has tip-toed around the topic. Indeed, spiritualism, while hugely popular, is a thorny issue. There are many who do believe – and whatever we write, we must respect those beliefs. At the same time, we aren't the sort of publication who indulges in cheap sensationalism."

"Do *you* believe?" I asked.

"The magazine's official position – which accords with my own – is that ghosts *may* be scientifically possible, but we will publish nothing without proof."

"And how would one obtain proof?"

"Why, we must see for ourselves. That is, if you're willing? I already have a medium in mind who's impressed a number of colleagues – and with your investigative skills, it should be a simple task to put her to the test."

"But why me?" I answered, half-alarmed, half-intrigued.

Smith isn't a man overly fond of emotion. "If you'll forgive me for being blunt," he said, "it seems that, if the dead are to speak, then they should speak to those who knew them best."

His words startled me, and I found myself struggling to keep my tone steady, my eyes fixed on his. "The medium is a *she*?" I replied, feeling I ought to say *something*.

"Yes, a delightful young woman by the name of Christine Burkins. I'll get my secretary to send over her address and some clippings from our files. She's making quite a splash."

"Shall I invite Holmes?"

"That's for you to decide. However, Miss Burkins' father is very protective. Should Holmes accompany you, then he may require additional assurances before he allows the séance to proceed."

"Additional?"

"Why, of course. What you report will greatly affect Miss Burkins' reputation. I have guaranteed that you will not interfere with the séance in any way and that, should you perceive anything amiss, Miss Burkins will be given the chance to respond, directly, before anything is published."

"In that case," I announced, in a hot rush, "let it be two weeks today."

We shook hands there and then and – all thoughts of lunch quite gone – I headed back out, into the heart of the city.

I was certain Holmes would dismiss the whole thing as tommyrot. Yet, since Mary's death, I'd frequently wondered whether we leave this world entirely once our spark has been extinguished, or whether some part of us remains to offer whispered reassurances in times of need. I'd considered what, if anything, would happen should I find myself sat, in a circle, calling out her name. I'd never had the nerve to do it, but I wasn't sure if I was afraid that there *was* something in it, or that there wasn't.

I walked in a desultory fashion, so occupied by my thoughts that I quite lost my way. Finally, finding myself in a warren of dark, claustrophobic alleys, I was gripped by a sudden, irrational fear. I recalled how, in *The Book of Samuel*, King Saul, desperate for guidance from the dead Samuel, conducts a séance – something God has strictly forbidden. And while he does indeed speak to Samuel, he's later condemned to death for his transgression.

Holmes had once said to me "work is the best antidote to sorrow," and I realized that work was exactly what I needed. Over the next week-and-a-half, I threw myself into my work in a way that I hadn't since Mary died.

It was Monday. The séance was in two days. Outside our window, autumn was putting on its best show. The day was warm and bright, with not a cloud to obscure a sky of cerulean blue. Yet, nothing – not even exhaustion – seemed to shake my mood.

"Out with it, my dear fellow!" Holmes suddenly said, seeming, as he so often did, to know my thoughts before I'd voiced them.

I was grateful for the prompt, but reluctant to admit my folly. "Oh, it's nothing. Nothing at all."

"Watson, I'd be a poor friend indeed if I hadn't noticed your mood. Why, for almost a fortnight, I've seen you reach for your pocket watch a dozen times a day, but never look at it – and Mary's likeness lying within. I've watched you smile at some remembrance, then seen your eyes mist over, and heard the smallest of sighs escape your lips. Come, Watson, on this week of all weeks, let us shake off this gloom. Out with it!"

"I'm afraid you'll think me rather foolish, Holmes" I replied.

"So, Smith persuaded you to go to Covent Garden then?"

"Why! How did you – ?"

"You returned from *The Strand's* offices in rather a brown study. As you hadn't eaten, I assumed Smith had given you the brush off, but it was soon clear that you had something more compelling than a missed rump-steak pudding on your mind. Immediately you returned, you pulled your old family Bible off the shelf and started pouring over something in the *Samuels*. You left the ribbon bookmark in place, so it was easy to find the exact passage you'd been so interested in. Given your recent loss, it's no great feat to put two-and-two together and naturally come to four.

"But Covent Garden? There must be a hundred mediums in London. How could you possibly know Smith wants me to visit one in Covent Garden?"

"Ah!" Holmes said, with a small smile. "*Mea culpa.* I glanced at the papers that Smith had delivered to you, as you read them over breakfast. Upside-down reading is one of the detective's oldest and most reliable tricks. Sorry, but you've been out on your rounds at all hours, buried in those journals of yours, and in between hardly eating or sleeping. Come: The cat's out of the bag. Let me refresh your coffee while you tell me all about it.

Holmes pulled up his chair beside the fireplace and began reading. He sat, pulling on his pipe for some time, checking and re-checking the clippings that Smith had provided, until he was thoroughly satisfied.

"Automatic writing, secrets revealed, materializations, mysterious knocking . . . It's all very compelling, isn't it?"

"I expected you to dismiss the whole thing out of hand!"

"I said it was compelling. I'm far from persuaded. Indeed, should you put me in a darkened room, I would immediately ask why is the room dark? For darkness has the potential to hide all manner of deceptions.

"Here – " Holmes jabbed his finger at one of the clippings in the manila folder and began reading: "*. . . the medium was removed to the bedroom, her head covered in a shawl to keep out the light and thus aid her in maintaining her trance. Shortly after, her spirit guide appeared and walked amongst us.*" I would ask what proofs are there that the medium remained in the room? Why does her head, not simply her eyes, need to be covered? Is it to hide the fact that she is, in fact, this wandering spirit?

"And here" – Holmes pulled out another clipping –" we have an account of objects apparating, but they always fall from *above*. I would ask: Could they have been tethered to the ceiling? Could they have been thrown by an accomplice?

"I do not say that trickery is involved. I remain, as ever, open-minded. But with reports such as these, much depends on what those present choose to see – or not see. None of these journalists question the events that took place. They're *watchers*, not *observers*."

"You'll come then?"

"If the father will have me. He seems to be quite the bulldog. What is it says here: "... *manages his daughter's career and protects her reputation as only a father can.*" I'd be curious to know exactly what that means. It sounds rather ominous.

"The real question, my dear chap, is: Are you certain *you* want to go through with it?" Holmes looked at me, his face the picture of concern, and I felt a great calm descend upon me.

"I confess, I find the idea unsettling, but I think I need to do it."

Holmes lent forward, regarding me with those singular eyes of his. "Well, then it's decided. On Wednesday, we will see what Miss Burkins has to show us."

I immediately telegrammed Mr. Burkins to inform him that both Holmes and I would be attending Wednesday's séance. Much to my amazement, I received a reply within the hour to the effect that, "*Sherlock Holmes and Dr. Watson will be most welcome.*"

"So much for the bulldog!" I glanced across at Holmes, feeling a warm certainty that, whatever surprises Wednesday held, I would not have to endure them alone.

"Excellent," he said. "In that case, I think a little reconnoiter might be in order."

"What do you have in mind?"

"Let us learn what we can of Miss Burkins and her father."

"You want to speak to the neighbors? Discover if anyone has seen accomplices rapping on the walls, or howling down the chimney?" I said, lightly.

Holmes chuckled appreciatively. "Stranger things have happened. But I suspect we'll learn a lot more about the young lady and her father from neighborhood heresay than from a folder full of yellow journalism."

Thus decided, we set out for Covent Garden.

Christine Burkins lived in a modest home above F.W. Collins and Sons, the ironmonger in Earlham Street. The Doric sundial which once stood at the intersection of the streets that meet at Seven Dials is long gone, but many of the houses in this area still date from the Stuart period.

The street is overshadowed by the Woodyard Brewery whose sights and sounds dominate – from the scent of hops roasting, to the noise of horse-drays clattering across the cobbles.

A hundred years earlier, this area was known as a place of dissent and political agitation, where the poor and desperate were crowded into unsanitary lodgings and left to rot. Today, the poverty is still there, disguised with a fresh coat of whitewash and an air of industrious purpose. Indeed, the streets that form Covent Garden's distinctive triangular plots are full of dark and narrow passages, an endless intricacy of courts and yards, with taverns, boarding houses, and workshops at street level, and homes above. Even during the day, it's a dangerous place. Or so we were to discover.

Holmes and I were making good progress, working our way along the street, chatting to passers-by, making enquiries about the Burkins family, without seeming to be too interested.

"I hear this place has its very own Oracle," Holmes said to a saw-toothed man who was setting up his barrow, and had paused to pull out his pipe.

"Stuff and nonsense!" the man said good-humoredly. "Such a sweet a girl too – How her pa managed to persuade her to be part of his flim-flam, I'll never understand."

"A bad lot?" Holmes prompted, offering the man some tobacco from his pouch.

The man sniffed at it experimentally and, clearly finding it superior to his own, began enthusiastically packing his pipe. "Ha! David Burkins is the man who gives the bad lot a bad name," he spat. "And he makes a very good living from fleecing fools too!"

"What's this, Pete? Playing that tune again?" A red-faced man, possessed of prodigious eyebrows, suddenly materialised. "Don't you pay no attention to Pete, here," he said, eying-up Holmes's tobacco pouch hungrily. "Him and Burkins have bad blood between 'em. Not saying he's a good man, mind. But that girl of his has the gift, right enough."

Holmes gave a little nod and, thus encouraged, Eyebrows helped himself to a fistful of tobacco. Soon, Pete and Henry – as the newcomer revealed himself to be – were batting it back and forth – their energetic debate punctuated by plumes of smoke, like steam engines taking a breath between underground stations.

"You said he makes a good living . . . ?" Holmes interjected.

"Ah, Pete don't know what he's on about. Why, if he does make money off the girl, you wouldn't know it. Both of 'em only have one decent set of clothes. Still, what if they do a little bit of the old flim-flam, as Pete says? Worse ways for a young girl without a muvver to make a living." Henry sniffed.

"So Burkins has no other work?"

"Laboring, hauling and shifting, casual, like a lot of us round here. He's brains enough. 'Book smarts', they say, before the drink got him."

"A drunk?" Holmes nodded encouragingly.

"A drunken brawler!" The man named Pete grumbled.

"Ah, life's took more than it's given of late, for poor old Burkins. So what, if he takes a drink? And so what, if sometimes he takes a drink too many, and talks too loud, and throws the odd punch at folk like Pete, here? He's always been a hot head, but since he lost his missus, it sometimes seems he's lost what sense he had too."

Tobacco – and gossip – exhausted, the two men finally returned to their work, leaving us to continue our stroll.

We were just about to turn into a passageway which afforded a better view of the Burkins' top-floor flat when Holmes grabbed my hand. "Watch out," he said. "Looks like company."

Ahead, I could see a short, brute of a man, holding a heavy stick, striding towards us with ominous purpose. I glanced over my shoulder to discover our way back now blocked by a rangy youth, wide-shouldered, with the build of one attuned to physical work.

"Gristle or fat?" Holmes whispered, his eyes fairly gleaming.

I nodded towards the stocky man. "Fat," I said. "Gives me something to swing at."

I've been in enough tough spots to know how to handle big, slow fellows like the neckless beast now roaring towards me. I steadied myself, and with my good ash stick raised, I prepared for his charge.

He was less than a foot away when I hit him. It had been many years since I'd played at single-stick, but I was delighted to find that the skills I'd learned at school, and polished in the army, hadn't deserted me.

True "gamesters", as they're called, keep their left elbow up, and advance with the right hand above and in front of the head, holding the stick across, so that the whole head is completely guarded. However, I had no time for such formalities. The aim of the game was to rattle your opponent's brains, and I went at him with all the dexterity the narrow passageway could afford.

"Why, I'll break you, an' that's the truth!" he bellowed.

Ho! I thought. *So you say! But I know this game better than you!* He came at me, trying to break my guard by virtue of strength alone. But single-stick is as much about speed and skill as it is strength. I caught every blow and returned it, like for like.

He was bigger than me, but shorter, and I used that to my advantage, reigning down blows on his knuckles and wrists until finally, with a curse, he dropped his cudgel. I caught him a smart blow on the chin, and another in the ribs.

He let out a wheezing groan and lunged for his lost weapon. *Too slow!* He backed away, winning himself another blow to chin, before he finally turned on his heels and ran.

Beside me, Holmes was doing steady work. Gristle was almost as tall as he was, with a reach the equal of his own. But compared to Holmes he was a poor pugilist. He telegraphed his punches so clearly that Holmes merely had to step aside to avoid them. Indeed, while I was too busy with my own entertainment to see much of Holmes's match, the proof of my friend's efficiency could be clearly heard in the echoes of blows landing.

With my own opponent finally disposed of, I turned to discover Gristle, red-faced and bloody-nosed, backing away down the passage way. I caught his eye and, seeing that it was now two to one, he let out a dog-like yelp and bolted. Holmes lunged at him, catching him by the coattails. The fellow let out another whimper, gave a curious shudder and, shedding his coat like a reptile sheds its skin, he vanished into the maze of Covent Garden.

There's nothing like seeing off ruffians half your age to put one in high spirits. Indeed, Holmes declared himself "quite delighted with the morning's exertions."

As for myself, although my muscles had already begun to protest, I found Holmes's mood infectious.

We decamped to the Café Royal, where we sat on red-plush banquettes and ate like warriors of old, our meal punctuated by tales of blows landed and blows dodged. It was only as we were taking our leave of Madam Nicols, who sits – French style – in her little glass-walled desk taking the money, that I wondered if our assailants had anything to do with the infamous David Burkins.

"It is a dangerous part of town. They could simply have been thieves. But if Burkins put them on to us, for what purpose?" I pondered.

"Indeed. If he intended to have us beaten enough to prevent our attendance at the séance – or to scare us away – then he'll going to be sorely disappointed. Still, it adds a little extra *frisson* to upcoming events, don't you think?"

I wasn't sure what to think, but I was content to enjoy a full belly, with the comfort of a pipe in front of the fire at Baker Street still to come.

Holmes spent the next day in the British Library's reading rooms, pouring through back issues of publications with titles such as *The Spiritualist* and *Borderland* in order to "get a feel for the common tricks mediums use."

He returned, early evening, clearly eager to share his findings.

"There's more to this business than I'd imagined" he said, stretching his back in a way that suggested many hours hunched over a table. "These publications treat spiritualism as some sort of new science, to be studied and tested. Why, there were just as many articles exposing frauds as there were extolling the virtues of some new, mystic prodigy."

"Oh? Learn anything useful?"

"I did," he replied, and began pulling assorted objects from his pockets: Several pairs of surgeon's rubber gloves, a pair of dark glasses, a yardstick, folded in the middle, some fishing line, and a set of pastel chalks.

"I picked these up at Harrods," he pointed to the gloves. "Apparently many mediums use their legs and feet to raise tables, tip chairs, and create rapping and scratching noises. So skilled are they that they can do so with the merest twitch and stretch – and yet their upper bodies remain static. Tomorrow, I will make a pair of rubber tourniquets from the gloves, and tie them around both legs, beneath the knee. I believe two hours should be sufficient for my legs to begin to swell. I will endeavor to sit next to the lady and, with my skin sufficiently tenderized, I should detect the slightest movement – no matter how skillfully done."

"Or you'll give yourself a thrombosis!" I protested.

"Fortunately, I know a fine medical fellow who will ensure I don't do myself any permanent damage!" he answered, laughing.

"Delighted to hear it. And the other items?"

"I shall wear the glasses tomorrow to accustom my eyes to the gloom of the séance room. The twine will be almost invisible in the dark – and will make a terrible trip hazard should anyone, unknown to us, attempt to enter the apartments after the séance has started. As to the other items, I cannot tell until we're actually there. We may assume that, if there is some trickery, Burkins will be working with his daughter. If so, there may be moments when I'll need you distract both of them. So when I wish to get to work, I will do one of three things: Sneeze, cough, or make some comment about the temperature in the room."

Holmes liked nothing better than a challenge, and a thrill ran through me as I recognized my friend of old – the Holmes I'd thought lost. Yet, almost as quickly, came the aching reminder of the loss that remained.

Sunset was half-past seven, and by the time we arrived at Miss Burkins' apartments, the gas-lighters were already on their rounds.

We found the street door open and wound our way, three flights, up a perilously steep staircase, at the top of which was another door.

Before we'd a chance to knock, the portal opened and a whiskered man, wearing a shiny suit, much worn about the cuffs and collars, appeared.

David Burkins was nothing like the man whose reputation had preceded him. He was tall and wide, with a strong handshake and a clear eye. Yet, I could see a tremor shake his muscular frame, and as he greeted Holmes, his voice broke. *Lord, I wondered, is it the drink or nerves?*

There was no hallway. The door opened directly into a small parlor whose shuttered window was covered in heavy drapes. The only illumination in the room came from a gas lamp in the centre of a large, round table – and the gas was turned so low I practically had to feel my way into the room. Holmes, I noted, moved with considerably more ease, having already adapted his eyes to the dark.

"Glad you could make it" Burkins said in a tone that suggested otherwise.

"We very nearly didn't," Holmes replied, "for we were in the area just a few days ago and were set upon by a pair of ruffians."

Our host raised his eyebrows, looking genuinely shocked. "*Crikey!* I'd heard some gents had a spot of bother. Thieves, was it?"

"They didn't say," Holmes replied cooly, giving the man one of his appraising stares. One thing was for sure: If Burkins had been involved in Monday's *contretemps,* Holmes would know, and he'd have every reason to feel uneasy.

A young lady was already seated at the table. I saw her rise to greet us, and a high timorous voice said, "I'm Christine. Please, make yourself comfortable. We have two more guests tonight but, hopefully, we will not make the spirits wait too long."

She'd barely finished speaking when I saw Burkins move to open the door again. Holmes seemed to take Burkins' movement as his cue, for he said, pointedly, "I find it abominably close in here, if you don't mind I'll take the opportunity to remove my jacket before we begin."

Holmes busied himself looking for somewhere to place his jacket, while I did my best to keep Miss Christine busy with small talk.

In the corner of my eye, I could see Burkins at the door, speaking with two young women, both dressed expensively and fashionably in rainy daisies and close-fitting jackets.

They spoke quickly and breathlessly, introducing themselves as "the Miss Clevertons".

The ladies had the attitude of children undertaking a dare who, as soon as their object is at hand, quite lose their nerve. For as soon as they had entered the little salon, their cheery chatter evaporated and they stood, hand in hand – all set, it seemed, to bolt at the slightest sniff of a spook or spirt.

Much to Burkins' chagrín, Holmes had already installed himself in the seat beside Miss Christine. "Come, sit beside me, Watson. That way, the ladies Clevertons will have the comfort of each other during the proceedings."

"Surely, Mr. Holmes, Doctor Watson, the ladies would prefer to have a gentlemen between them in case of distress?" Burkins protested.

"Oh, I think there's nothing like the reassuring hand of a sister in times like this," Holmes responded.

"You're so right!" the ladies chorused, gratefully.

However Burkins seemed determined to rearrange the seating, and there followed a verbal tug-o-war, with Holmes smoothly countering every objection.

It was Miss Burkins herself who put pay to the debate. "Don't make a fuss, Pa," she said. "The spirits don't care who sits where. Now, if we're ready, I'll dim the lamp. Please don't be concerned. I will not leave you completely in the dark. Pa, if you'll light the candle – the spirits much prefer it – then we will take each other's hands."

As the gas was extinguished, I heard Burkins, who still stood, sentinel-like, near the door strike a match but, wherever the candle was, it cast such poor light as to make little difference to the gloom.

Almost immediately, Miss Burkins began her invocations, inviting the spirits to join us. "Miss Cleverton," she said, "who is it you wish to speak to?"

"Our Aunt Agatha" they replied in unison.

"Mr. Holmes, who is it you wish to speak to?"

"My grandmother," he said, much to my surprise.

"And Doctor, who is it you wish to speak to?"

"Mary," I answered. No sooner had I given my reply, then I had a sudden revelation, which was so shocking it made me cry out.

"Why, Mary is here!" Christine said – and indeed she was, for I could smell her perfume!

"She will answer your questions if you ask," Miss Burkins said.

My mind was in such a riot that I barely knew what to say. "My dearest? Is it really you?"

I heard a voice, then, whispering in my ear. It sounded faint, muffled, as though someone was speaking from far, far away. "*Yes . . .*" came the answer.

"Does today mean anything to you?" I asked, barely able to keep my voice steady.

"*Sad . . .*" came the reply.

That day – the day I'd deliberately chosen for the séance – was my birthday. It was a day that Mary and I always celebrated with friends and much laughter. Why would she think it "*sad*"? Her reply made no sense! But I must understand!

I attempted to calm myself and think. *Was she sad that she could no longer share it with me? Or was death the cause of her sadness?* I had been so wrapped-up in my own pain, it hadn't occurred to me that the dead, too, may feel grief! I was about to ask more when I realized that I could no longer feel Holmes's cool, reassuring hand resting on mine. I felt a movement, beside me, fast and sudden, followed the sound of a hollow slap, and a clattering noise as of something falling.

The ladies Cleverton gave terrified little yelp.

"Don't be afraid," Christine said by way of explanation. "The spirits are with us, and you may hear and see things tonight that cannot be easily explained."

I could still smell Mary's perfume, but it seemed that she was unable to answer any further questions. I tried several more, until finally, Miss Burkins told me what I feared – that the veil between us was too heavy – that she could not break through.

"Don't be disheartened, Doctor. It sometimes takes time for a loved one to learn how to speak to us" she explained. "Let us try Agatha. Come, Agatha, will you not speak with us? Anna and Jane are here."

"Yes, yes," came the voices of the ladies Cleverton, "are you there, Aunt?"

For a moment all was silent. Then, without warning, there came a dull thud from above.

The ladies gave a delighted squeal, for apparently the spirts choose to communicate in many ways, and tonight Agatha was making her presence known with taps and raps on the ceiling.

"Oh, my dear, how we've missed you!" the ladies chimed. "We've come for your advice. Anna has had an offer of marriage. Should she accept? It's from dear James Mathers!"

Another dull thud followed, which the ladies took as a vote of confidence for the intended. More questions quickly followed – Should Anna wear the silk or the satin? Should she invite her hated cousins to the wedding? Should she choose a spring or a summer date? – until it seemed that the ladies' entire future was to be determined thus: One rap for yes, two for no.

Once again, I noticed that Holmes had released his grip from mine, and once again I felt a movement, beside me, fast and sudden, followed the sound of a hollow slap. Then another, and another.

The ladies seemed oblivious to the noise, but the loquacious aunt – perhaps chastised by some spirit, impatient to speak – suddenly fell silent.

Despite there still being "a million questions we have to ask," Anna and Jane professed themselves delighted with their evening – apologizing profusely for, as they said "monopolizing the spirts" and insisting that "dear Mr. Holmes must have a go."

It was at this point that Mr. Burkins appeared beside the table. He whispered something to his daughter and, with her apparent acquiescence, he leaned across to relight the gas.

I noticed, as he did so, there was a strange red dust on his hands and around his lips. I glanced at Holmes, whose hand was now back in mine, and saw the whisper of a smile cross his face. Of course!

Now that I knew – or at least guessed the trick – I felt a bolt of anger. By God! Smith would have his article, and Burkins and his child would never again be able to play on the misery of others.

Still, the evening wasn't over, and despite my ire, I determined to say nothing until the final proofs had been gathered.

"It's been suggested," Miss Christine said, "that, in order to contact Mr. Holmes's grandmother, we attempt automatic writing. I confess this is something I've rarely tried. One clears the mind and writes the first words that come to mind – guided by the spirit's hand. It isn't exact, but we will try it."

Burkins placed a sheet of paper and some ink on the table. The gas lamp was turned to full, and for the first time that evening I was finally able to see exactly what sort of person Christine was. Like her father, one wouldn't have known by looking at her that she was a liar and a fraud. She was young, fair-faced, with a wide-eyed look that, had I not known better, I would have taken for honesty.

"I'm ready," she said, closing her eyes, pen in hand. "Mr. Holmes, ask your questions."

"I only have one and it is this: *Si tu es là, grand-mère, s'il te plaît, écris ton nom sur le papier.*"

The silence that followed Holmes's unexpected question was priceless! We sat there for many minutes, Christine's hand poised over the paper, but no matter how many times she entreated the spirts, Holmes's grandmother didn't write her name on the paper as requested.

The ladies Cleverton had taken their leave, and Miss Christine had retired to her room to rest, leaving just Holmes and me with Burkins in the little parlor.

With the ceiling gas jets lit it was difficult to imagine anything supernatural could ever have happened within these very drab, very ordinary walls.

I knew Holmes had much to reveal, and I was just as keen to hear what he had to say, as I was to give Burkins a piece of my mind. Yet what he said next took me completely by surprise.

"I must apologize, Mr. Burkins," Holmes began matter-of-factly. "I had no intention of interfering with tonight's performance. Ghostly chatter about fiancés and weddings was enough to test the most patient man – and I'm not that! – but

I'm afraid I quite saw red at seeing my friend so sorely abused. 'Sad' was a good guess, for many people visit mediums on the anniversary of their loved one's death. It was not, I suspect, the answer the Good Doctor expected, and his distress as he attempted to make sense of it was palpable." He materialized the foldable yardstick from his sleeve and, with a snap of his wrist, flicked it open. "I do hope I haven't done you any serious injury?"

Burkins looked like a man lost at sea. "I knew I was taking a risk letting you come, Mr. Holmes. But things are getting out of hand, and I'd rather be exposed by a gent like you than some Fleet Street hack. If I've gotten a few raps across the knuckles tonight – well, it's no more than I deserved. But what the Hell is this red stuff?"

"Just a little pastel chalk, Mr. Burkins. I had the occasion to examine the room while you were greeting the Miss Clevertons. There were two things that struck me as out of place in a parlor used for best: A broom, and a three-foot spool tube of the type used inside rolls of cloth. Both were suggestive, so, I marked them with chalk, if case anyone should touch them, knowing the red wouldn't be visible in the dark.

"I must say, it was well done. The violet scented candle was a nice touch. Violet is one of the most popular ladies' fragrances – and most will know someone who uses that scent. I only have one question: *Why?* It's clear your daughter knows nothing of the deception, for it would have been much simpler to have her tap on the table with her knees. She could have had the tube between her knees, too, and moved it with her feet into a position where she could speak into it by merely lowering her head. Yet, she did neither. Indeed, she barely moved at all.

"Switching to automatic writing was a good gamble, too. The skilled medium quite naturally picks up clues about her sitters during the course of an evening, and guided by her subconscious, may write things that seem insightful or prescient. If not, no matter, for the willing participants of a séance will find truths in the merest scribble. Yet, Miss Christine made no attempt to fake a reply to my question.

"No – I know the *how*, but I cannot fathom the *why*. You aren't even making any great profit from the exorcise, despite the interest of the press and society ladies like the Clevertons."

Burkins let out a long, slow breath. "Lord! I never meant any harm. It was me – all me. I felt so lost after my Paulette died, and someone said that Mrs. Williams over in Soho had the gift. So we went along – me and Chrissy. And, well, Mrs. Williams said all the right things. Said Chrissy had the gift too. And so Chrissy starts up with the Ouija board and the cards. And she got so distressed that her Ma wasn't speaking to her, so I sort of helped things along . . . And that just made things worse . . . ."

"And people heard about it?"

Burkins nodded sadly. "What could we do? Chrissy was so happy. And we made a bit of money – like you said, not much, for Chrissy doesn't like to profit from the spirits' good will. And one thing led to another, and me having to find more and more ways to keep the illusion working, like . . . But I guess now you'll write your article, Doctor, and me and Chrissy will be branded frauds and thieves. Lord!" he cried, tugging at his beard distractedly. "What if they put us away?! What if they set the law on us?"

As Burkins spoke, I felt my anger ebb away. Here was a man who had lost his love and lost his way. It didn't seem fair to press more losses upon him. "Don't worry, Mr. Burkins, I'll give my editor my apologies. Tell him I changed my mind and won't be writing the article after all. But it would be best if you discontinue before, as you say, some hack writes what I will not. How will you manage it? What will you tell Christine?"

Burkins looked from myself to Holmes before shaking his head determinedly. "I'll think of something. Tell her it's time to let the spirits rest, maybe."

"I think," Holmes said, "that's a fine idea." I saw Holmes, once again, quietly appraising the man before adding, "Now, if you will excuse us, while it isn't yet nine o'clock, given the Garden's reputation – and our recent tussles – we'd rather not linger."

It wasn't until we were on the street that I asked, "Burkins didn't set Fat and Gristle on us, then?"

"I think not."

"So what now?"

"Well, given that it's your birthday, I was about to suggest The Albion. And I think, if you're willing, we might speak of Mary?"

"I think" I said, linking Holmes's arm in that way that friends do, "I would like that. I would like that very much."

NOTES

• "Calamity" Smith was the pen name of Herbert Greenhough Smith, editor of *The Strand* magazine, 1891-1930.

• The Albion tavern, at 26 Russell Street, opened in 1829 and was demolished in the 1920's to make way for the Fortune Theatre. According to Charles Eyre Pascoe, writing in 1892, it provided its customers *"with a thoroughly home-like English dinner, which costs, with a moderate quantity of light wine or ale, from three shillings to five shillings"*. Like many public houses of the period, he notes that the "dining-room is never honored with the presence of ladies".

• The hugely-popular Spiritualism movement has its origins in the United States in the 1840's. It was based on the belief that the spirits of the dead can communicate with the living – and offer them insights into the human condition. As the Victorians viewed themselves as living in a progressive and scientific era, many spiritualists sought to cast ghosts and spirits in terms of scientific possibility, rather than something mystic and unknowable.

• "Colleagues" may include Watson's editor, Sir Arthur Conan Doyle, who is known to have attended séances in his youth and would later become a notable champion of the Spiritualist movement.

• In 1 *Samuel* 28:3-25, King Saul approaches a medium for advice from the dead Samuel, in direct opposition to God's prohibition. According to 1 *Chronicles* 10:13, Saul later died because he "*was unfaithful to the Lord*".

• F.W. Collins and Sons were a legendary London ironmonger. The business was at 14 Earlham Street from 1835-2008.

• The Seven Dials area of London features seven streets which today meet at a roundabout with a sun dial in its centre. The dial only has six faces, with column itself acting as the seventh dial. The current sun dial was put in place in 1989 replacing the original, which was removed in 1773 and (despite London council's attempts to repatriate it) is still kept by Weybridge Council.

• To avoid asphyxiating passengers, early steam-powered underground trains had to "hold their breath" between stations, and were provided with regular "breathing holes" along their routes.

• Single-sticking was a popular martial arts, which began as a way of training soldiers and marines in the use of swords in the 1700's. It last appeared as an official Olympic sport in 1904.

• The Café Royal, at 68 Regent's Street, was established by French wine-merchant, Daniel Nicols, in 1865. By 1895, it was being run by his widow, Célestine. It was widely considered to have the best wine menu in London.

• Rubber surgeon's gloves were invented in 1889-1890 and used to protect doctors' hands from abrasive detergent. Interestingly, Harry Houdini used the exact same tourniquet trick in 1924, as described in his "Margery" Pamphlet. In it, he details his attempts to debunk a spirit medium known as Mina Crandon, who was a contender for the $2,500 prize offered by Scientific American magazine to any medium who could produce *"conclusive psychic manifestations"*. As Sir Arthur Conan Doyle and Houdini were friends, it's likely he learned of the technique from Doyle.

• Rainy daisies were style of walking skirt popular with sporty young ladies in the 1890's.

• In "The Adventure of the Greek Interpreter", Holmes mentions that his grandmother was "a sister of Vernet, the French artist". Although he never specifies which of the artistic Vernet brothers, given the resemblance between Horace Vernet and Holmes, it's likely that his grandmother was Camille Françoise Josephine Vernet (later Camille Le Comte).

• Watson was born on 7 August, 1852. This, in 1895, would have been his forty-third birthday.

An UnChristian Act

"So much for *The Daily Chronicle*," Holmes said, dropping the paper on the floor with a sigh.

May 1895 had started warm and breezy, with a promise of a glorious summer ahead. Alas, it seemed that Mother Nature had other plans. By Thursday the sixteenth, thick smoky fog had moved in. A flurry of snow fell overnight, turning day into night and the streets outside into an ice-rink.

So it was that Holmes and I found ourselves gloomily wrapped-up against the weather, when we'd much rather have been wrapped in sheets, enjoying the dry heat of our favourite Turkish bath.

I sat in silence for some minutes, weighing up the effort of retrieving the newspaper against moving from my warm spot beside the fire.

The Chronicle was one of the better dailies, with a reputation for fair and factual reporting. I had no doubt, however, that the main reason Holmes read it was for the extensive personal advertisements it carried.

"Any insights?" I asked languidly, secretly longing for some excitement to shake me out of the morning's funk.

"Let me see," Holmes replied with a yawn, "*CAD* is utterly brokenhearted, promises that all can be made right. *BUNCLE* demands inviolable secrecy. *IPR* offers proof of good intentions with a letter to *CG*, in Paris."

Knowing my friend's knack for unpicking these opaque missives, I knew he wouldn't miss the opportunity of demonstrating his skills. "Oh?" I prompted.

"*CAD*, as the lady no doubt playfully dubbed him, is Charles Arnold Delabole. Once heir to the Delabole slate fortune, now down on his luck, and linked to the rich widow, Lady Farriers. This, despite being engaged to the very beautiful but penniless *chartreuse,* Marianne LaBrea. *CAD* indeed!

"*BUNCLE* is a Scot's dialect corruption of Bonkyll – referring to Bonkyll Castle in Berwickshire – ancestral home to our dear Queen's current *aide-de-camp*. A visit to the old homestead is unlikely to require inviolable secrecy. Nor, indeed, a personal ad. I'd warrant, then, that Her Majesty is planning a trip to the Scottish Isles.

"*IPR* is clearly my dear rival, Ignatius Paul Pollaky. How curious. Old Paddington Pollaky, as he's known, used to specialize in intelligence on aliens living in Britain. I understood he'd retired. I wonder what's tempted him away from the comforts of Brighton domesticity?

"Still, there's nothing of especial interest to us here, although maybe the mail will offer more inspiration?"

I'd often thought there was something preternatural about Holmes. He could see, hear, and smell things that were simply invisible to mere mortals like myself. But that morning, his abilities appeared all the more remarkable for the seeming lack of effort required to employ them.

True to his prediction, Mrs. Hudson appeared in short order, carrying the morning's mail on a silver tray, with the promise of hot cocoa to follow.

It wasn't unusual for Holmes to receive upwards of a dozen letters daily. As for myself – I rarely received correspondence. My life was in London. I had no family, and friends did not need to write, for they saw me often enough to dispense with the effort.

Holmes worked his way through the little pile of mail with a series of *Hmm*'s and *Ha*'s. I watched as he picked over the contents of each letter before they were crumpled into balls and tossed into the fire.

"Missing dogs, errant husbands, wayward sons . . . *comme d'habitude*! At least there are none those unwelcome social summonses which call upon a man to lie and invent some prior commitment. If you were hoping for an excuse to escape Baker Street today, my dear Watson, then I'm afraid there's nothing . . . Ho, hold on! What's this?"

There was something about his tone that set my heart pumping.

"For you," he said throwing me the last letter on the tray. "Don't dally now. I swear my mind has been so starved of late that I can almost taste a mystery here. Look, now – have you ever seen an address written with such force? The nib has gone through the envelope at the end of each line, and the ink has pooled so much on the last line that he's likely to have snapped the nib entirely. Your well-connected friend in Dorset must have had quite the shock, and been at his desk before dawn."

I looked at the envelope and saw that it was postmarked at half-past-seven – Whoever had written it must have been awake very early – or very late – to catch the first post of the day.

I opened the envelope, feeling the heavyweight paper which had given Holmes the clue to its sender's social status. By the time I had unfolded the message within, my hands were shaking with anticipation. Holmes was right – there *was* a mystery here!

"Good Lord!" I cried in surprise. "It's Tadpole Phelps – you remember, Holmes? That Foreign Office affair with the missing papers, some four or five years ago?"

Holmes shot me one of his keen, questioning glances. "Indeed! Go on."

I read the letter aloud before passing it to Holmes, knowing that he would be able to squeeze every ounce of meaning from the remarkable letter that Phelps had written.

Watson, [it began]

It has been some time since we spoke, and I hope that life has been as good to you as has to me. You'll recall my mater-

nal uncle, Lord Holdhurst, whose preference for me was always the subject of so much teasing in school? Well, the poor fellow died two years ago, and I was left his sole heir. I'm now firmly ensconced in the family pile, a Member for South Dorset, and Justice of the Peace to boot – if you can imagine that.

I confess that the 'Tadpole' you knew at school would have laughed at the thought of so much responsibility falling on his bookish head, but I am determined to prove my worth and show the naysayers that my uncle's faith in me was not misplaced.

This evening, however, has tested me sorely and, as JP, people are looking to me for reassurance and answers.

There has been a murder, Watson! And one so strange and shocking that I worry how the town will respond once all is known. For the sake of our old friendship, I write to ask that you and Mr. Holmes come as soon as you receive this letter which, by my reckoning, will be first post.

I will instruct a carriage to wait at Swanage Station and check every train, so that you can be brought to Studland without delay. As I write, the boy is waiting to catch the post, so I will save details for our meeting.

Please do not fail me.

Your old school-fellow,
Tadpole Phelps

I glanced at Holmes and saw that familiar look of suppressed excitement being kindled. "Excellent!" he said. "Excellent! Just what the doctor ordered. Now, where's that *Bradshaws'*?"

Studland is a sleepy sort of place, nestled between Poole Harbour and Studland Bay. To the south lie the Purbeck Hills – a hog's-back of a ridge, half-a-mountain high, and beautiful in its windswept desolation.

To the north are the mossy carpets of the Bagshot Beds. Follow the sloping heathland down towards the sea, and the curious traveller will eventually reach the ever-busy harbor, where fishing boats jostle for elbow-room with steam-packets, wooden dingys, and pocket cruisers.

Studland village lies in the southern curve of the bay and is the only sizable settlement in these parts. It's a pretty village comprising rows of heavily thatched cottages, lined up along pressed-dirt lanes, which wouldn't have looked out of place in the time of Shakespeare. Within the village, there are few buildings of any note or distinction besides the manor house and the Church.

The house was built as a villa and much enlarged by Lord Holdhurst's parents to create a rambling sort of place whose charm lies in its apparent unplanned confusion. Part one-story, part two-story, part gabled, part hipped, with a mess of turrets and chimney stacks, diamond-pattern windows peek from beneath the slate roofs, like tired eyes. Untamed gardens festooned with wild flowers add to the charming quality of the whole.

In contrast, the church of St. Nicholas – to the east of the village – has that square solidness of design that characterizes early Norman architecture. The building is fortress-like in appearance, reflecting the violent past of this now sleepy headland where raiders from the sea were once frequent visitors.

From Waterloo to Swanage took us six hours. At Wareham, a new branch line wound its way across towards the coast before reaching a delightful stone-built station, which looked more like a cozy cottage than a busy seaside terminus. It amused me to note that the word "*Swanage.*" on the running board had a large full stop at the end, as though to dissuade any arguments to the contrary. Or perhaps it was to indicate to travelers that, here, modern comforts ended. For, to progress any further, we would have to endure the bumps and bruises that are part of the package when one travels by carriage on country roads.

On the platform, we were greeted by a gentleman sporting a fulsome Mexican mustache and a hat a size too big, and chosen, presumably, to accommodate his prodigious ears.

Charteris, as the macrotia-blessed individual proved to be, chatted amiably as he escorted us to the carriage. We settled in while he telephoned Phelps, grateful to find that blankets had been provided to insure us against the cold.

When our driver returned, he refused to be drawn on the events of the previous evening, saying only that he had instructions to take us directly to Studland where Phelps would be joining us.

We were delighted to discover that old Tadpole had also provided a hamper, which we attacked with the eagerness of two men who had missed breakfast.

Inside the hamper we found a veritable *smorgasbord* of sandwiches – beef and curry-butter, egg and chutney, celery cream, cod's roe – along with bottles of fiery ginger beer.

We also found a copy of the morning newspaper, with a report circled in pencil and a note scribbled in the margin, declaring:

The local news hounds have beaten you to the chase. But be assured that the scene is secure. I await you arrival.

Phelps

"Good grief!" Holmes cried. "Look at this, Watson – " And he handed me the newspaper.

Considerable sensation has been evoked in the town of Studland, Dorset in consequence of a body found on top of the Agglestone at the southern end of Studland Bay. Disturbing reports link the death to the discovery of a number of foot-tracks of a most mysterious description.

On Thursday night, there was a very heavy fall of snow in the neighborhood. The following morning, inhabitants were surprised at discovering the tracks of what they took to be someone running barefoot towards the cliff tops that lead to Handfast Point and Old Harry's Rocks. The prints were to be seen in all kinds of inaccessible places, including the tops of houses, and inside walled gardens. The tracks progressed in a series of long strides or hops, and it was upon following them that locals discovered the body of a yet-unidentified young woman.

That great excitement has been produced among all classes may be judged by the fact that the victim was found on top of a stone long associated with pagan sacrifices and unChristian acts. The Justice of the Peace, Mr. Percy Phelps, MP, has assured residents that investigators from London have been called, and will be attending within the day.

"'*Pagan sacrifices*'?" I said, digesting the article along with the remainder of my sandwich.

"Well, as I've often said, the vilest alleys in London are less terrible than the isolated beauty of the countryside. Give me an honest East End villain over a sequestered community any day!"

"Surely not!" I said, suddenly feeling protective of Tadpole's little slice of England.

"I'm in deadly earnest. Look around. What do you see?"

I wiped a circle in the condensation on the carriage window and peered out. "Why, nothing but wild spaces and nature."

"Exactly," Holmes said. "No one is ever really alone in a city. There are eyes everywhere. Not all of them are friendly, to be sure, but most are. Even the direst rookeries contain good people, willing to do the right thing. But here? A body could lie undiscovered forever, with no one to claim it. And while in a city the weight of public opinion can be mobilized to fight for justice, in places like this, the law is often little more than some Baskerville-esque tyrant."

"You can't mean that!" I spluttered. "Besides, Percy is hardly some tyrannical lord of the manor."

"Oh?" Holmes said, a whisper of a smile growing across his face. "Well, perhaps we'll make an exception for Phelps on account of his good taste in friends. But I warn you: Should we end up being sacrificed to some pagan god, then I'll hold you personally responsible."

I chuckled along good-heartedly but as the coach rattled along the narrow lanes, I could see the news report begin to work its own peculiar magic on Holmes. Soon, he had adopted that far-away look, and all conversation was lost.

I, too, could not help but dwell on the newspaper article. We were racing towards a new century – and such superstitions belonged in the past. But then, the growth of spiritualism in recent years had proved that, no matter how sophisticated our world had become, there are always those who find comfort in the unknown. If man can evolve, then, so too, can he devolve.

Thus occupied by our thoughts, it seemed no time at all before we arrived in Studland. The carriage had barely stopped when the door was thrown open – and there was Phelps himself, his pinched, pale-face looking eerie in the glow of the carriage lantern.

"My dear fellow!" he cried, pumping my hand like a thirsty man pumping for water. "You came? What am I saying? Of course you would, of course you would!" He turned then to Holmes and said, in the same excitable tones, "Mr. Holmes, thank goodness! Come, come, the crowds have been growing by the hour, and more snow is expected. You must see it. The full horror of it, before busy feet and the weather obliterates everything."

The particular stress that he laid on the word "horror" made my stomach lurch. I could see that Holmes, too, was alarmed by the urgency of Percy's speech.

Despite the cold and the snow, which still lay thick from the previous evening, it seemed that the whole village had come out to witness the events that had befallen this tiny community. People stood in the doorways of barns and cottages, small groups huddled together under mighty oaks, and a few eyed Holmes and me with a curiosity bordering on hostility.

But for the most, their attention was focused on the thin line of armed men who stood by, guarding the church.

The militia that Phelps had employed to keep the "scene", as he put it, clear of interference had certainly done their job well.

At this time of year, it wouldn't be dark for few hours yet, and the footprints mentioned in the newspaper were still perfectly visible.

Indeed, it would have been impossible to miss them. The tracks were small enough to have been made by a child. In some places, only the barest imprint of toes could be seen, as though someone had been running, pell-mell on tiptoes. In other places, one could see the imprint of the whole foot, buried deep in snow – sometimes one foot, sometimes two – so that it seemed like someone had been playing hop-scotch. No human child, however, ever could ever have left such footprints behind. They appeared and disappeared with huge gaps between each step. Prints appeared halfway up walls, on the side of houses, and most remarkably, over the ridge of the church nave.

Phelps led us through the line of militia towards the church. Holmes had yet to say a word, and Percy quickly gave up his desultory attempts at conversation.

We could see the vicar and another man nervously poised in the arched porch of St. Nicholas's, awaiting our approach.

Finally Holmes broke his silence. "Well done, Mr. Phelps," he said warmly. "You've done a splendid job here."

"I did what I could," my old school friend replied, in that quiet, nervous tone he had. "I'm afraid I couldn't stop the whole village from going about their business, but the vicar was willing to keep the church closed up until you had the chance to examine the prints. They run through village, across the boundary wall, over the church roof, through the churchyard, then on, towards the heath. I've more men posted along Heath Green Road and at the Agglestone itself, where the body still lies."

Holmes nodded. "And when were the prints discovered?"

"Around eleven o'clock yesterday evening by Mr. Bastin. Here he is now. The portly chap beside him is our vicar, Reverent Merchant."

"Portly? Whose portly?" A round, smiling face emerged from the shadow of the stone archway that covered the door.

Introductions made, we quickly retreated inside the vestibule, but not before Holmes's keen eyes had spotted something of interest.

"Ah, you've noticed our corbels, have you?" the vicar said, waving a pair of chubby hands to indicate something presumably running under the exterior roofline. "Everyone does. Those medieval stone masons were a scandalous lot. The ladies they carved must have been contortionists! Of course, our parishioners get in quite a stew about them, but, it's just ancient history."

"Pagan?" Holmes asked.

"Some believe so," the genial gentleman replied, blinking furiously. "The old beliefs hung on longer than many like to believe. And some of them seem to be older than the current building, suggesting they've been imported from some more-ancient structure. But I'd say they're playful rather than pagan."

"Not everyone agrees?"

"Oh," Merchant's smile broadened, "I'm forever having to stop irate mothers from knocking lumps off them. Mrs. Eggins – she's my housekeeper – keeps sewing valances to cover them up. Thankfully the wind here is more persistent that she is. They never last the night!"

Holmes glanced back towards the churchyard, where neat little headstones were crowded up against stubby trees, which had been bent by the wind into curious shapes. "Interesting," he said, although I wasn't at all sure he meant the valances.

A tall man stood beside the vicar looking like someone who wasn't used to so much scrutiny. "'Now, then Mr. Bastin," Holmes began, "what can you tell us?"

Phelps gave the vicar a nod, as if to free him from any injunctions that had been laid on him. The vicar responded by giving Bastin a gentle tap on the shoulder and, as he did so, I noticed how, despite his calm tone, his hand trembled.

Bastin reacted like a racehorse at the starting whistle – galloping through the events of the previous night as though he'd explode if he didn't tell everything he knew immediately.

"It were around eleven," he said in that lilting accent Devon folk have. "I'd spent the evening in the Bankes Arms. It were busy, and we'd all stayed longer than intended, on account of the weather. The snow came in around nine. Then the wind, which were already strong, whipped up sumut awful. About ten, I heard this strange sound, like sumut being dragged down the street. Now, this area has a reputation. They say piskies dance on the rooftops come nightfall and, true or not, no one wanted to go out and see what the matter were."

"Piskies?" I interrupted.

Bastin looked at the vicar and licked his lips uncertainly.

"What Tom means are the fey. This area is full of legends – the Agglestone, on the hill, was said to have been thrown here by a giant. And the hill itself is named after Old Nick. But piskeys are the souls of children who died without being baptized. I'm afraid that the early Church had no shame at all. They used all sorts of underhand tactics to convert people to Christianity!"

"I see!," Holmes said in a low, excited whisper. "Please, go on, Tom."

"It were near eleven when we finally trooped out. I started up the road. There were plenty of cloud, but they were movin' fast, and the moon were cumin into its last quarter – big an' bright – so, I saw 'em straight away. Footprints. Toe prints really, as though from dainty little feet.

"In some places, the snow were all smudged, and I had a fancy that whoever made 'em had been twirling around, like doing a jig.

"About 'alfway up the lane, the prints vanished and I backtracked to the inn, to see if maybe they'd gone another direction, but there'd been so many comings and goings, there were no way to tell.

"I headed back the way I came – my farm is just past the church, see – and sure enough, the footprints started up again. I'll be honest, Mr. 'Olmes, I'd had a few, and at that moment, I quite fancied catching myself a piskey or two. They might not be Christian, but fairy ladies are said to be mighty pretty. But then I saw those footprints up high, on the church wall, and then on the roof, and I lost my nerve. Ran hell-for-leather into the church, where the vicar found me, and thankfully let me sleep off my drunk. Felt right foolish, too, until I heard about the body and figured I'd done right to stay on Holy Ground!

"You were there when they found the body?" Holmes asked, turning his attention towards Merchant.

"Why, yes," the vicar answered, "but how did you know?" He refused to meet Holmes's steady gaze, instead fussing over his his cassock, as though plucking off imaginary lint.

"Forgive me, but you've the air of a man who's had a terrible shock," Holmes said gently.

In reply, Merchant gave the ruddy-faced farmer another tap on the shoulder. "Tom," he said, "I think if Mr. Holmes is agreeable, you can go back home now."

I was sure that Bastin would rather have stayed on Holy Ground, but he shrugged manfully and headed out of the church. No sooner had he left than the vicar visibly deflated, that odd, forced cheerfulness, quite vanishing.

"You're right Mr. Holmes, it's been terrible! But Tom and most of the villagers only know the barest details, and Percy has been keen to keep it that way. I know you'll want to view the body before the weather closes in, but we've a few hours yet, and if you'll come through to the sacristy, there's a kettle on the fire. What I have to tell needs at a good strong cup of Ceylon.

"There aren't many youngsters in these parts," Merchant stated. "The girls get sent into service, and the lads to the factories or the boats. Those who have no offers or money to move away quickly get into trouble. That's why I've started to use the sacristy in the evenings. I can keep an eye on the church better from here.

"I was here last night, reading beside the fire, when I heard a hellish commotion. It started suddenly – a low, desperate wail, followed by the clatter of hobnails on stone.

"I expected to find youngsters riffling the poor box, or breaking up the pews for firewood. Instead, I found Tom, flat on his face, eyes wide, mouth opening and closing, but no sound coming out, save for pitiful whelps.

"I helped him up, dusted him down, and filled him with tea. But it wasn't until the second cup that he dared tell what had spooked him so.

"In all honesty, I thought he was seeing shapes in the shadows. But I'd heard a noise myself, earlier, over the rooftop, so I thought it best to go investigate.

"I saw the prints instantly. But it was a curious thing: My lantern flicked and gutted, and the clouds overhead did the same, so that in that juddering light, it appeared that the footprints were actually moving.

"That fairly froze the blood in my veins, I can tell you! But I reminded myself that even if piskies turned out to be real, a portly man of the cloth was unlikely to be of any interest to them.

"I followed the tracks out of the churchyard. On reaching open ground, you cross into a lane which leads to a winding track, then a forested area. I was certain our night-time visitors must have returned to whatever woodland glen they hailed from because I lost the trail there. Still, some instinct told me to press on.

"I crossed the footbridge, which takes you to a narrow path that skirts the woods, and ultimately leads out, onto the heath.

"The path itself is treacherous, with patches of boggy furze and hidden hollows that will break your ankle if you aren't careful. My progress was painfully slow, but I picked up the tracks again at the point where the heath starts to curve up, towards the Agglestone.

"The rock is a giant wedge, shaped much like an anvil, and rises from the centre of an amphitheater of bog, dotted with clumps of cotton grass, crisscrossed by rivulets.

"Its name comes from the Anglo Saxon *'alig'*, meaning *'holy'* - suggestive of an ancient pagan site, which time has turned into something ominous. I had always dismissed tales of human sacrifice, of blood rites, and evil – until that very moment.

"First I saw that mass of prints in the snow, just in front of the stone – caused, I believe, by some frantic last minute struggle. Then, I saw *her*.

"That poor child, laid on top of that dreadful slab, dressed in sacrificial gowns. Her ankles and wrists were bruised, where she had been tied down. Her head was twisted, her eyes staring, and there was that wicked, raw, red gash across her throat, where some fiend had bled her dry."

So affected was I by the vicar's speech that I could think of nothing to say, but Holmes was never one to stand on ceremony.

"There was blood at the scene? You saw that?"

"No, but I assumed the snow had covered it."

"Was the girl covered in snow?"

"Why, no, no . . . ." Merchant said, stammering now. "But the wind could have blown the snow off."

"Her throat was definitely cut, though?" Holmes insisted. "You saw that?"

"Not then. But Percy had ladders taken up later, and that's what it looked like."

"Mmm. So, you went straight to Phelps to report what you'd seen?"

"That's right," Percy said, his voice heavy with anxiety. "Knocked me up around one. I called the local constable, and we three went up. It was the constable who arranged for men from the neighboring villages to be brought in as guards, until you'd had a chance to see everything."

"No doctor?"

Phelps shook his head.

Holmes looked at me. His face was a mask, but in the firelight of that little stone room, his eyes looked like they were ablaze.

The evening was bright, crisp, and clear. The snow lay on the heath, as thick as goose-down. Everywhere, blue marsh flowers and white asphodel glowed as our lamps glinted off the hoar frost that lay on the blossoms.

I recalled how Homer had described the Greek Meadow of Death as covered in asphodels, and found myself shuddering.

Holmes walked beside me, his head bowed, his eyes fixed on the those pitiful little footprints.

As we reached the dip that led to the Agglestone and our own meadow of death, the winds rose, making our little cortege stumble in the boggy earth.

Just as Merchant had described, the tracks ended before we reached the rock itself, but it seemed to me that, rather than a struggle, what we were seeing was some strange dance. What was it Bastin said? Like someone doing a jig. "What do you make of it?" I asked Holmes.

"Interesting! And did you notice how the trees hereabouts have been bent by the dominant easterly winds? Yet, as we get closer to the Point, the winds start to plunge over the cliffs, creating swirling back-eddies."

"Is that important?" I asked.

"Watson, it's the key to everything. But a look at this poor, dear girl will fill in the details we're so sorely lacking."

Made of sandstone, the Agglestone must have been at least thirty feet high, and several hundred tonnes in weight. Yet its entire bulk was balanced, unfeasibly, on one small point and, stretched out on its flat surface, lay the body of a young girl, dressed in white, her skin as pale as the surrounding snow. Never had I seen a more mournful nor uncanny sight.

The ladders that Phelps had brought up to the stone were still in place. Holmes and I gingerly claimed one apiece, and began to examine the child.

"No blood," Holmes noted.

"No – none. What Merchant took for the mark of a knife seems to be the imprint of a rope of some kind."

"Strangled?"

"Garroted would be a more accurate description, given the deep neck abrasions and the hemorrhages on her skin. It's hard to be sure without a more thorough examination, but her neck may be broken. But look, here, Holmes! Look at the way she's lying, the position of her body. It's almost like she's been dropped from some higher point. Unless you believe in giants, that's hardly likely. Could she have climbed up herself?"

"The footprints we followed are undoubtedly hers. But the last visible tracks are at least four foot away from the base of the stone. She couldn't have been carried and placed here, because there are no other prints. She certainly couldn't have jumped up. How indeed? But see here," Holmes continued, distractedly motioning to the abrasions around the girl's legs and feet. "There are no marks on the skin to imply she was held or tied down. No indentations from fingers, or trace fibers. But, given these bruises on her feet, I can see why Phelps might have thought that.

"So what do we have? The bruises curve over the dorsum. I hate to speculate, but given that we're working in straitened circumstances, I'd say they're from shoes. Not the usual ankle boots that a girl might wear for every day. Something showy and fashionable, with a high tongue, like evening pumps. That would account for shape of the bruises. Especially if they were too small, and chaffed at her feet. Perhaps she borrowed them from a friend because they matched her dress? Then there are the smaller cuts and abrasions on her legs, arms, and face, almost as if she'd been walking through thick undergrowth . . . ."

"But there *are* rope marks on her wrists," I said.

"Yes, but given that we need these very long ladders to even view the body – Who could have tied her down? And there's nothing to tie her to. I'd suggest she was holding onto something, rather than tied to something. Or tangled in something Yes! That's the ticket!" Holmes added in a sudden, excited rush. "Yes, yes!

"Now, look at her clothes. These aren't sacrificial robes. This is the lady's Sunday best. See the ribbons in her hair? Made from lengths of serge – offcuts – in navy blue. The exact blue, and the exact material, used by the British Navy. And the Royal Navy Base at Nothe Fort is almost exactly due east. We have it, Watson, we have it!"

It took Holmes two hours, waiting for replies to telephone calls and telegrams to confirm the details – and what a sad story it was.

On the morning of Thursday the sixteenth, fourteen year old Mary Williams, dressed in her only good dress, with navy ribbons tied in her hair, and a pair of striking blue velvet pumps borrowed from her young cousin, climbed onto a trapeze bar strung beneath a giant kite, outside Nothe Fort, Weymouth, Dorset.

The Fort had been built as a coastal defense in the 1860's to protect the Royal Navy Base at Portland and the kite's inventor, Jennings Wilcott, hoped his demonstration would help sell his "war kite" to the navy.

Wilcott's idea was that "spotters" could be sent aloft, and trained to identify enemy troops to warn of an impending attack.

On the day of the demonstration, thousands of people gathered to watch the ascent and descent. "A companion and I stood on the harbor," said the reporter from *The Weymouth Telegram*, who was just finishing the story for publication when Holmes telephoned. "We had a fine view of both the kite and of the girl. The kite was a large contraption, constructed of a series of rectangular boxes, stung four in a line, and attached to a winch on the ground with a long rope. The girl, Mary Williams, was in comparison tiny – seeming like a doll besides the kite.

"She was a local girl and, indeed, had many friends in the crowd who spoke glowingly about her pluck. It was said she'd recently lost her position and was hoping the flight would make her fortune, and many were there to cheer her along.

"The wind had been high all day. The kite rose quickly, and the spectators thrilled to see the girl lifted so high above the Fort. Then, suddenly the wind dropped, the kite fell, and we feared she would be unseated.

"But she stayed up, and a great roar went around the crowd. This seemed to encourage the man on the winch, who let out more rope, allowing the kite to climb even higher than before.

"By now the wind was coming in stronger, and there were cries for her to be pulled back in. We could see the girl was struggling to remain on her seat, but the man – Mr. Jennings Wilcott – shouted up to her to not be afraid.

"However, the crowd was getting restless. It was wrong, people said, to take advantage when she was so young. Others said that she was always headstrong, and if things went bad, she only had herself to blame. Thankfully there were more for her than against her, and once again, the cry went up to bring her down. And, once again, Wilcott remained unmoved.

"The girl had been up almost ten minutes when there was a terrible noise, as of tearing cloth and before our eyes the top portion of the kite disintegrated, like wet paper.

"Wilcott panicked and in his rush to reach the winch, he knocked the bar which locked the remaining cable in place. All we could do was watch, in horror, as the rest of the rope unspooled, setting the kite to fly free.

"The girl did indeed have remarkable pluck. While the women on the quayside cried and howled, she remained calm. We could see that she seemed to be working her arms and feet, as if trying to steer the thing out to sea. If she could have landed in the water, then she would have been safe. And it seemed she would have her way. But then, at the last minute, the wind took her – and she could not resist.

"The kite bucked and shook, and for one horrible moment, it looked like it would break apart entirely.

"The wind eased off again, and the crowd gave another cheer, but it was quickly seen that something was wrong. In her attempt to maneuver herself away from land, she had become entangled in the kite strings. 'Oh Lord, she's dead!' said someone in the crowd, but by then the kite had been carried over the Fort and quickly vanished."

A week later, Holmes and I were sitting in the drying room of our favourite Turkish bath on Northumberland Avenue. It was over a smoke, lying on a couches, that I spotted the coroner's report on the front page of the morning's newspaper.

The inquest on Mary Williams had concluded the previous day, and had ruled that the deceased had *"accidentally died, when the strings of the kite which was carrying her wrapped itself around her neck. It appears,"* the coroner was quoted as saying, *"that Mary Williams' body was dragged some thirty miles across country, before the bobbing kite was caught in crosswinds. As the ropes that she was caught in untangled, her body was deposited on top of the Agglestone rock in Studland. It is assumed that the remains of the kite was carried out to sea."*

In his summing up, the coroner added, *"We wish to censor Mr. Jennings Wilcott, showman and inventor, in that he showed great carelessness and disregard for the safety of such a young girl by allowing her to attempt the ascent without proper forethought or training. It is recommended that Mr. Wilcott be prohibited from carrying out further demonstrations until suitable reparations are made to Miss Williams' family."*

Thinking about how cruelly the girl had met her end, it was a small comfort know that we had, at least, been able to ensure that the truth about her death was known.

"No, Watson, it's no comfort at all," Holmes said, sadly, reaching for the pouch of tobacco secreted in the inside pocket of his coat, "Mary Williams is still just as dead. You may call me a fool, but when it comes to murder, give me an honest cutthroat any day, for it seems infinitely more horrible to die at the behest of someone looking, as our American cousins would say, to get rich quick, than at the hands of some unthinking hothead."

"How is a cutthroat any better?"

"He isn't. But while the cutthroat goes to the gallows, accepting the penalty for his crime, Wilcott gets to go to dinner parties and plan his next escapade, in the full knowledge that there will always be someone desperate enough to take the risks while he takes the glory."

NOTES

- According to the Meteorological Office's weekly reports, 16th-17th May did indeed see a sudden cold snap that brought snow and thundery storms.
- *The Daily Chronicle* was considered a liberal newspaper, carrying regular features on striking workers, Irish home rule, and what it called "Greater Britain Day by Day" with news from the Colonies. It was one of the first papers to popularize small personal adverts, which were often written in coded language.
- In the late Eighteenth Century, ownership of Bunkle Castle passed to the Earls of Home, meaning that the aide-de-camp Holmes mentions would be the 12th Earl, Charles Alexander Douglas-Home.
- Ignatius Paul Pollaky (1828-1918) was a contemporary of Holmes. His offices were at 13 Paddington Green – hence the nickname. He retired in 1882 but, if Holmes is right, then it seems that he remained active in the business – at least unofficially.
- In Victorian London, postal deliveries were made at least twelve times a day in most cities. The first delivery was at 7:30 a.m., the last one at 7:30 p.m.
- The Foreign Office affair that Watson mentions was in 1889 – six years, not four or five years earlier.
- *Bradshaws' Railway Companion* was a timetable book that became an indispensable item for regular travelers – so much so that *Bradshaws'* became a household name.
- Studland Manor House is as quirky as Watson describes. It is now a National Trust property.

- Period photos show the Swanage Station running board does indeed have a full stop, which was strange enough for Watson to note.
- The end of the Nineteenth Century saw a growth in spiritualism. Secret societies, such as The Hermetic Order of the Golden Dawn, promoted occultism and magic, blended with esoteric eastern philosophies. This was seen as a reaction to Darwinism, and the search for "meaning" and spiritual certainty. Max Nordu was a doctor and social critic who argued that such spiritualism was proof of the degeneration of the species. His book *Degeneration* was published 1882-1883, so Watson was certainly keeping up with his reading.
- The corbels of St. Nicholas's Church are famously pornographic, including several *sheela na gigs*, and some very acrobatic couples!
- The Agglestone fell onto one end and side in 1970 and is no longer the distinctive anvil shape Watson describes.
- The use of kites in warfare dates back to ancient China. Victorian interest in aeronautics, and its practical applications for warfare, revived the idea. In the 1820's, British inventor George Pocock developed the first modern "man-lifting" kite, using his own children in his experiments. Expositions in which inventors would demonstrate balloons or kites became hugely popular, and often involved hoisting young girls into the air – the ladies being both lightweight and offering a certain glamour to the proceedings.
- Aeronauts continued to use young girls in their displays. Just a year after Watson's account, another fourteen-year-old girl, Louisa Maud Evans, died when the balloon she was in went out of control. She did have a parachute, which she used to jump to safety,

but she fell into the Bristol Channel and was dragged under the water by the weight of the chute. Until the invention of airplanes, parachutes were generally only used by acrobats, who performed stunts on a trapeze bar suspended from a descending chute.

• The type of kite that the journalist describes seems to have been based on the box kite invented by Lawrence Hargrave in 1885. His design used four box kites tethered together, and it could lift an adult man. The American, Samuel Cody, and Captain Baden Fletcher Smyth Baden-Powell (brother of the Scout leader) also developed their own kites for aerial observation. Cody's "Man-lifter War Kite" was adopted by the War Office Balloon Companies of the Royal Engineers in 1906.

The Violated Grave

It was a cold, breezy December morning. The season had London firmly in its grip, and the usual riot of carriages and hawkers on the street outside had been silenced by the frost. The blinds were still drawn against the boisterous weather, and Holmes and I were settled on either side of the blazing fire, enjoying the lethargy that comes to busy men who suddenly find they have nothing urgent requiring their attention.

I had been flicking, half-heartedly, through the newspaper when a curious headline caught my attention – *Mummys' Curse Strikes Again!*

"Well, well," I chuckled, glancing at Holmes, who lay curled up on the horsehair sofa, pulling contentedly on his pipe.

The article mentioned Dr. Winter, who was something of a legend in the medical fraternity. The venerable gentleman had honed his craft in the days when doctoring was learned via the violated grave. In the last sixty years, his techniques had progressed little beyond bleeding and cutting – Indeed, it was said that he still regarded a stethoscope as some "newfangled French toy".

During my time at Barts, Winter had become a byword for every type of bunkum and quackery. I'd imagined him long dead, so it was with some surprise that I saw, beneath the improbable headline, the name of the same "Wooden-Head" Winter.

Holmes glanced at me, languidly. "Someone you know making the news?" he asked.

For a reply, I threw him the newspaper.

"Dr. Winter – a body snatcher from the time of the old king," I said in way of explanation. "He was quite notorious when I was a student." I was just about to launch into an account of some of the more outrageous tales attributed to Winter when Holmes gave a strangled cry and sat bolt upright.

"By Jove!" he cried, jabbing his finger at the article in an attitude of intense excitement.

Suddenly, the listlessness occasioned by a cold day and a warm fire vanished. Holmes had an uncanny nose for a mystery.

"Why, whatever is it?" I asked, my nerves tingling to the sudden thrill in Holmes's tone.

"'*Strange Death at the London Polytechnic...*'" Holmes began reading. He galloped through the first part of the article which, despite the headline, detailed the events of the previous day in a surprisingly sober tone. "Ah, now, here we are . . . ."

It was as Dr. Winter was undertaking a necropsy of an Egyptian princess that a member of the audience was struck down by a series of violent fits which were to claim his life. Constable Jones of H Division was called to the scene, where he saw the body and pronounced life extinct. *This death is not the first to be attributed to the so-called "Cursed Mummy". Indeed, the princess has been linked to numerous uncanny events since she was removed from her resting place in Luxor, Egypt.* Constable Jones deposed that the gentleman was between thirty to forty years of age, possibly of Italian origin, and may have been an entertainer. The deceased's likeness is reproduced here. Anyone able to assist with identification is asked to contact the Coroner at the City of London Mortuary.

"I'd warrant," my companion said in an excited whisper, "that the gentleman was discovered to be wearing embellishments of some sort. The police see an entertainer. I see a disguise."

"Recognize the man?"

"It isn't a face I've ever seen, but he bears similarities to someone who has recently been brought to our attention," Holmes replied enigmatically. "It's strange that the article makes no mention of an inquest, but I begin to suspect why."

I knew better than to press Holmes for an explanation before he was ready to share his thoughts. Instead, I asked if he intended to contact the coroner.

"Indeed. I'll telegram ahead. What of your Dr. Winter? Any idea where he might be found?"

"None. Years ago, he was appointed head of the Barts branch of the British Medical Association, but he turned in his notice after the first meeting, if you can believe it. It was all bit too new and fast for him! Still, if he's still in practice, they'll have his details. I'll find out."

Holmes opened up the window and leaned his lean frame out into the frosty morning air. His hawkish eyes scoured the street below. I saw him give the flicker of a smile and wave his hand. A clear high whistle came in reply to the summons and, within minutes, I heard the ring of the street bell, Mrs. Hudson's distinctive sigh, followed by the clatter of youthful feet on the stairs.

Simpson is one of what Holmes calls his "Baker Street Boys".

My colleague employed a seeming menagerie of street urchins to run errands and find the unfindable, for the princely sum of a shilling a day. This particular scrap of mischief was as lean as a greyhound, and twice as keen. His face quite fell when he learned that Holmes merely wished him to send telegrams, rather than track down some errant villain. However, a shiny coin in his pocket quickly brought the smile back to his face.

"Want me to wait fer replies, Mr. 'Olmes?" he chirruped in that cheery Cockney way his breed employed.

"If you would, please."

Simpson vanished, leaving us to make a leisurely breakfast while we waited for the boy to return.

My friend busied himself loading his plate, in a way that showed that an energetic fit had quite superseded the apathetic one. As for myself, I found Holmes's mood contagious and ate with relish, looking forward to what the day would bring.

"So, this Winter chap," Holmes prompted, clearly keen to indulge my desire to share my reminiscences. "An Egyptaphile?"

"Probably just checking up on one of his old patients!" I laughed.

Holmes chuckled appreciatively. "'*Necropsy*' is an interesting choice of terminology," he said.

"Yes, very Winter-ish. If the word *necropsy* was commonly used, he would surely adopt the term '*autopsy*' by preference. This is a man who utterly rejected Germ Theory. As for Natural Selection, it was said he would laugh himself to tears at the very mention of it!"

I was just about to entertain Holmes with the story of Sir John Sirwell's gaul stone when Simpson re-appeared with not two, but three, telegrams clasped in his grubby hand. "I let the girl know I'd wait and take anyfink that came across the wires for you," was his explanation.

I had witnessed Holmes insult royalty to their face, yet he always spoke to the lowliest beggar with the utmost courtesy. It wasn't that he was a political animal, but he had a strong sense of natural justice. He couldn't abide the cruel, arrogant, or inept, but any man or boy who was useful, hardworking, and intelligent was sure to win his approval.

"Excellent, excellent!" Holmes said, offering Simpson an additional coin for "his diligence".

The urchin scampered off, looking mightily pleased with himself as Holmes shuffled through the telegrams.

"You know, Watson, I've often marveled at Brother Mycroft's uncanny ability to know what is *happening* without ever leaving his armchair, but this verges on the supernatural."

He passed over a telegram to me to read, which I reproduce here:

To: Mr. Holmes, 221b Baker Street, NW
Received at 10:15 a.m., December 2nd, 1895

Strongly suspect Italian to be French gentleman, last of Campden Mansions, Notting Hill. Friends of England await your report, as do I.

Mycroft

It was only a few weeks earlier that Holmes and I had been engaged in the Cadogan West affair. Surely "the French gentleman" referred to was one of the foreign agents who Mycroft had suspected of involvement in the case?

"The name you're struggling to recall," Holmes said, seeing my furrowed brow, "is Louis La Rothière."

I picked up the newspaper and looked, once again, at the face of the dead man. "What did Mycroft tell you of him?"

"I've no doubt he has extensive files and photographs, but all he gave me were the broadest brushstrokes: Keen sportsman, athletic build, skilled marksman, mid-thirties, brown eyes, dark complexion, aquiline nose, and, most usefully, 'a long scar under the chin, from a knife wound'."

"It's quite impossible to see his chin with that soup-strainer he's wearing," I said, peering at the sketch of the heavily bearded man with renewed interest.

"That in itself is suggestive, given the current fashion for men to be clean-shaven. Still, it doesn't do to speculate before all the facts are known." Holmes glanced through the remaining correspondence before passing the document on to me to peruse. "While Mycroft's involvement will doubtless muddy the waters, the one thing we do now know is why Winter was invited to take part in the *'necropsy'*".

I looked at the address and noted with amusement that, according the Medical Association, Winter lived literally next door to the Polytechnic!

Holmes had also received a reply from the coroner. "Where to first?" I asked.

My companion hummed distractedly, as though weighing up the options. "With weather such as this, we can be fairly certain that, if Winter's still in practice, he won't be too busy. The City Mortuary, however, is always busy, especially this time of year."

His logic was as sound as ever and, having decided to make Winter our first port of call, we donned our Ulsters, and five minutes later were in a hansom, driving furiously for Regent Street.

In his pomp, Winter must have been an impressive specimen. In his eighth decade, he was still remarkably vigorous. His face was browned from the elements, and his hair was brindled with flashes of pure white, so that he looked more magpie than man.

We were ushered into Winter's neat little consulting room, where he sat, glowering at the world, as though ready to catch malingerers in the act.

"Come, come!" he cawed. "And don't forget to close the door, lest the germs get in!"

"Dr. Winter," I said, "it's very good of you to see us."

"Not at all. Molly mentioned you're here to talk about the chap who died at the necropsy? Terribly bad show. Didn't even get to unwrap the old gal."

Holmes gave an curious, choked cough, "Yes, I see, Doctor. I can imagine that must have been . . . frustrating . . . Perhaps you could talk us through the events of that evening? Any detail – no matter how small – will be of immense assistance."

The doctor rang for Molly to bring brandy and, thus fortified, he settled down to tell his tale.

"This sort of thing was all the rage in my youth," he said, by way of introduction. "People went mad for anything Egyptian – and it was quite fashionable to watch a mummy being unwrapped. Of course, it was done very respectfully. Chap would always give a little talk about the history and what-not, before you got down to the bandages and bones.

"Mind you, people then weren't as squeamish as today's lot. You'd pass around the bandages, fish out any trinkets. Ladies always loved those. And then, of course, there'd be the chance to eat some of the flesh – "

"I'm sorry?" Holmes said, shooting me a look of alarm.

"*Mummia*, you know?" Winter replied, as though eating the corpses of dead Egyptians, in the belief they medicinal properties, was the most natural thing in the world to do.

"Ah!" Holmes nodded. I could see the humor in his eyes, but his face was the very picture of studious attention. "And you've done a number of these 'unwrappings'?"

"Oh, dozens!" Winter said, airily. "But this was the first time I've encountered one with a curse attached to it."

Again Holmes nodded, his face appropriately Sphinx-like. "I rather thought this sort of thing had fallen out of fashion."

"Absolutely. Haven't done one since old Brummell died. But I'm always the first port of call whenever anyone at the Polytechnic needs anything of a medical nature. And when the history fella there was offered the chance to examine the mummy that's been causing everyone so much trouble, he could hardly refuse."

Now it was my turn to express surprise. "Trouble?"

"Accidents, apparitions. To hear people talk, you can't even look at the thing without chinaware flying across the room, or dogs dropping dead."

Rather stumped for anything else to say, I followed Holmes's lead. "Ah! I see," I said. "Please, do continue."

"My thought immediately was that the fella who owned it wanted to offload her. She might be a princess, but there have been too many scare stories. He couldn't sell her now for any amount of money. He'd clearly decided the best way to realize his investment was with a public lecture."

"If I may ask," Holmes interrupted, "do *you* believe that the mummy's cursed?"

"Not saying I do. Not saying I don't. But if a man lives long enough, he sees *things*."

"You weren't worried about performing the necropsy, then? That it might . . . *precipitate something?*"

"Did I think she'd curse me? *Ppfft*. Let her try. I'm an Englishman!"

"But a man did die."

"Yes, but he was *Italian*. Still, it wasn't a natural death – not at all."

I could see that Holmes wanted to ask Winter what he meant, but the doctor was clearly a man not be rushed when he was spinning a yarn.

"Jenkins had just given his talk on Ancient Egypt, and I could see the audience were already half-asleep. Dull as ditchwater, that Jenkins, so I quickly stepped up.

"Back in my youth, a party wasn't a party without some form of entertainment. Old gypsies would do the rounds telling fortunes, magicians would conjure up lightning in bottles, mediums would spew out ectoplasm. The best trick I ever saw was a spiritualist who sold her whole act with some patter about science. The more she banged on about science, the more people expected something uncanny to happen . . . I've used her exact words at every unwrapping. Works every time!

"'Ladies and gentleman,' I began, 'we're here in the pursuit of *science*. Whatever you see tonight, please remember that science – *and science alone* – has the answers . . . Now, what we have to show you this evening is the body of a young woman who died three-thousand years ago, preserved using arcane methods, long lost to time. Her body was hidden so that she could sleep the sleep of the ages, undisturbed. Alas, that was not to be – for here she is, transported from the tomb of her ancestors to this dusty hall.

"'You will all have heard of the curse. You will have heard how those who removed her from her resting place died, their bodies wracked and bloodied. You will have heard that whenever anyone attempted to put her on display, the glass on her case would shatter. You will have heard how moans and sobs have been heard to emanate from her sarcophagus. You may even have heard how, when her photograph was first taken, and when the plate was developed – although the negative hadn't been touched in any way – it was seen that, imposed over the bandaged face, was the image of a living woman, whose eyes stared furiously at the viewer with an expression of singular malevolence!

"'If you believe in spirts – if you believe that the dead have power over the living – then I ask you to leave now, for this is a place of *science*."

As Winter spoke, he'd risen to his feet, quite wrapped in his memories, gesturing to Holmes and me as though we were the audience and the desk between us was the mummy. Then he paused, seemed to recall himself, and sat back down, chuckling.

Winter looked from Holmes to myself, his face creased with silent laughter. Knowing him by reputation, I couldn't help but wonder what he found the more amusing – the sideshow patter he was dishing out, or the appeal to *science*.

"I could hear little thrills run through the audience" he continued, collecting himself, "so I knew they were ready, which is when I asked for volunteers to help me take off the first layers of wrapping.

"Usually I'd expect a couple of young bucks to come forward, looking to prove their courage. But no one did. Like I said, this generation is soft – namby-pambies, the lot of them. Anyway, I was standing there scissors in hand, ready to do the necessary on my own, when this chap bursts in through the side door and plants himself right beside the mummy. *Ho-ho!* I thought. *Here's a man after my own heart after all!*

"Side door?" Holmes asked.

"Yes. The hall has two doors. The one at the top of the tiered auditorium, where the audience usually enters, and one in the stage area, that's used to move equipment from storage, without having to negotiate the steps.

"Well, the chap was followed in quick order by the doorman – apparently he hadn't shown his ticket. Well, I wasn't about to let some silly argument over money steal my thunder, so I told him to leave us be.

"I started clipping at the wrappings and asked my volunteer to hold the scissors. I wasn't sure he had heard me because he just stood there, sort of gulping, over and over, his eyes fairly popping out of his head.

"I guess he wasn't as brave as he imagined, because he was as jumpy as a cat, covered in cold sweat. Then it happened. He put his hand up to wipe his forehead, and suddenly there was blood everywhere. His face, his hands. Someone in the front row screamed – and that was when the ladies started fainting."

"Blood?" Holmes interjected. "Was he cut? Please be as clear as possible, Doctor. This is very important."

"Didn't get a proper look. By then that damned doorman, Brown, was on him, like a dog worrying a bone. He'd grabbed the man by his sleeve and was pulling him away from the mummy. All the time, the chap was jabbering something – sounded like Italian – *Tué! Tué!* There was this awful tug-of-war going on. The man's face was covered in blood, the ladies in the audience were getting more and more distressed, and Brown kept yabbering about '*No ticket!*'

"Then suddenly, someone screamed, and that set off a stampede. There was an almighty rush for the doors, and I had to cling onto the mummy to stop her from being knocked to the ground and trampled. I fear that I may have oversold the curse a little. For a while, all I could see were bodies pushing and shoving. When the crowds cleared, I could see the doorman had finally noticed something was amiss. He was white as a sheet – and I'm not surprised. Our chap was standing there, mouth opening and closing like a fish gasping for air. He had this curious stiffness of posture, face tight, jaws clenched, as though he was already dead. You see that sort of thing often enough, you know what's coming. And sure enough, he dropped like a stone. By the time I could get to him, the poor fellow was on the floor, convulsing so badly I thought he'd break his back.

"What did you do?" I asked.

"All I could do was try and hold him down, to stop him injuring himself. But the fits came in waves, one after another, and within in fifteen minutes he was gone."

"Did you call for help?"

"I sent the doorman to find a constable."

Having already formed my own conclusions, I asked Winter what he thought had caused the man's death.

"An aneurysm. Given how he gawped at the mummy, I wouldn't be surprised if the chap had scared himself to death."

"When you made your examination, were you able to discern where the blood had come from?"

"With an aneurysm, a nosebleed would be most likely."

"But you said, you didn't see any blood until he wiped his forehead?"

Winter shrugged his huge shoulders. He could easily have smeared the blood from his nose across his face."

"And how close to the mummy was he? Could anything on the corpse have affected him?" Holmes asked.

"No, there was no decay to speak of. No strong miasmas at all."

"Mould?"

"None."

I thanked Winter for his time, feeling, I confess, a little nonplussed at the man's lack of rigor. "Well," I sighed as we walked towards the street door, "at least the miasmas didn't kill him."

"Indeed," Holmes barked out a laugh. "They haven't killed anyone for a couple of decades now."

Being so close to the Polytechnic, we took the opportunity to speak to the doorman who, after the bootless errand at Doctor Winter's, proved refreshingly helpful.

The man could have been Simpson grown to adulthood. Wiry, with keen eyes, he fairly jumped to attention when Holmes asked him about the "Italian gentleman".

"Lord, it's murder then?" he said, eyes widening. "I thought as much. He came in here, all red-faced and panting. At first I thought he was just another student running late – they always are, you know? But then, when I saw that blood in the lecture hall, I knew someone had done fer him."

"You saw him come in?" Holmes asked, regarding the man with his steady grey eyes.

"Not exactly. I heard the bell over back door. Lots of students use the tradesman's entrance, see. I'm a cyclist myself, and I let them leave their bicycles in storage for safekeeping. I walked through to see who it was, but he was already heading for the lecture hall – ran right past me. He'd left the back door ajar and I could see his bicycle outside, so I brought it in. Then I realized I hadn't seen his ticket and, this being a public lecture, I couldn't let that pass."

"When you went outside, did you see anyone?"

"Wasn't looking. But if anyone was running after the gent – if that's what you're suggesting – I'd have heard them. These backstreets echo so."

"Where did you find the bicycle, exactly?"

"Just beside the door, but if you're wondering where he was coming from, then there are only two routes that are any good for city bicycling that lead here – traveling east from Cavendish Square, or west from Smithfields.

Holmes asked to see the bicycle. It was resting amongst an assorted jumble of boxes and scientific equipment, and it was some time before it could be untangled and brought out into the light.

I'd lost count of the number of times I'd seen Holmes stretched out on the floor, magnifier in hand, in order to better examine some vital piece of evidence. Yet the spectacle never failed to interest. As I watched him examining first the pedals and then the wheels of the bicycle – sniffing at this and that – I wondered what clues he would uncover.

"No grass," he said eventually "but lots of mud and slurry. Smithfield Market, I'd warrant. And, see here, blood on the handlebars. Our man was attacked and pursued, of that I've no doubt. But why did he come here?"

"Well, Mr. 'Olmes," the doorman said thoughtfully, "south from Smithfield, you can ride hard and fast, following the Thames, as far as you like. But if I was being followed, I'd want to go north – lose myself in the mess of the city . . . and these backstreets are right warren, and no mistake."

"That's an excellent hypothesis, Mr. Brown. Just one more question: Did you hear the gentleman *say* anything?"

"Lord he was jabbering, but I don't have the lingo. Let me think. '*Metuee*', sounded like."

"Wonderful! Absolutely wonderful" Holmes grasped the doorman by the hand, and pumped it so effusively I feared it would fall off. "Thank you, Mr. Brown. You've no idea how helpful you've been."

Provision for the dead, in a city of five-and-a-half million, has long been a subject of debate. Thirty years earlier, it wouldn't be unusual for the poorest families – often living in one room – to be compelled to spend weeks with the corpse of a deceased loved one before he or she could be interred. It was fear of disease that finally forced the hand of the authorities.

One could still find taverns co-opted into use as Coroner's Courts, and tiny backstreet hovels used as makeshift charnel houses, but the City of London Mortuary was a veritable palace of the dead. With *post-mortem* rooms, a disinfecting chamber, ambulance station, and Coroner's Court, it represented the very best in modern medical and criminal practices.

We were quickly introduced to Mr. Ellis Thompson, Surgeon, who, despite looking quite knocked up, greeted us warmly.

He explained that the season, foul weather, and general illness had caused something of a backlog – to wit, no autopsy or inquest had yet been carried out on our questionable Italian.

I was surprised. An inquest would normally be called almost immediately. And, it was usual, if death occurred with a medical practitioner present, for the doctor to be asked to carry out the *post-mortem*, unless he was implicated in the death. "Dr. Winter wasn't asked to perform the examination?" I asked.

Thompson shrugged his shoulders, flicking through the paperwork with an attitude of confusion. "You are Dr. *Watson*?" he finally asked.

"Yes . . . ."

"Well, don't ask me how or why, but it seems that *you* are to undertake the autopsy."

"But we only telegrammed a few hours ago."

"I'm aware of that, Doctor. But see – here's your name on the order."

Holmes shot me a knowing look.

"Mycroft?" I asked in amazement.

"It would appear so," Holmes replied, his eyes sparkling. "Do lead on, Mr. Thompson. At least we'll be able to reduce your backlog by one."

If one is accustomed to it, there's no mistaking the smell of death. But the *look* of death – that's something that's unique to each individual. I've seen women eaten by cancer who, on their deathbed, appear decades younger, as though, in those final moments, they had somehow shed the suffering they'd endured. I've seen stillborn babies whose faces bore such a look that one might imagine they'd stared into Hell itself. Murder victims are no different. While a body can carry the most appalling wounds, the face may look as peaceful as if the dead person was asleep.

This is why poison is such a popular method of murder. For while the effect of poison on the living body may be savage, upon death, it's often only possible to prove wrongdoing by a thorough *post-mortem* examination.

This wasn't the case with body we were tasked with identifying. Such had been the strength of the spasms and choking that preceded death that the evidence of it was writ large on the face – and body – of the man who lay on the cold marble of the mortuary table.

Neither Holmes nor I needed to open the body to know the cause of such a violent death. Only one poison made its victims convulse, and eventually asphyxiate in such a way: *Strychnine*.

We approached the dead man in the usual way. First we looked to the posture. The back was twisted and the hands and jaw clenched, which was consistent with our supposition of strychnine poisoning. The room was so cold that there were thankfully no unpleasant odors, other than those that the body had gained in the last hours of life.

"Almond oil and rose water" Holmes noted. "Likely cold cream." He took another deep breath, his nose hovering only inches away from the body. "Chalk and bergamot – that will be face powder. There's a hint of orris root, too, which is used in rouge. So, our victim has indeed used embellishments to change his appearance. Ah – interesting. Orange notes and – Ah, ah – petitgrain. Our man favors Orloff's Special Cologne – a Russian perfume. It would seem that our man has recently been to Russia.

"There's one more scent too: *Sweat*. Given what we know, that shouldn't be so surprising. In the final hour of his life, he exerted himself enough to perspire freely."

"What about the strychnine?" I asked, pointing to the signs of dried liquid around the deceased's mouth. "Ingested?"

"Possible, but I think not," Holmes replied, pointing to the rows of angry cuts on the back of the man's hands. "Defensive wounds. Very deep. And here, too, purple welts on the calves of each leg. Interesting and – Ho! What's here?"

The man's right hand seemed to be clasped around something small, so that we had the terrible task of breaking the fingers in order to see what it was he was still guarding, so carefully, in death.

The object in question turned out to be a silver key, which Holmes examined before putting it to one side.

The body had already been stripped, and the key now joined the rest of the man's possessions.

There was only one more thing that was needed to confirm the victim's identity – which Holmes was able to do by feeling for the long white scar that ran just beneath his beard.

I glanced at Holmes whose eager eyes told me everything I needed to know.

"Louis La Rothière?"

"Yes," Holmes, said, "and his story is almost complete. Now, let us fill in the gaps. What else do we have here? A small coin purse, a leather wallet with gilt mounts, a Hunter pocket-watch – he was a sportsman – a silk handkerchief, and a platform ticket from Liverpool Street Station. The clothes are clearly of French design. There are no labels, but the cut is very distinctive. And, here, in the pockets of his jacket – gloves. The color – tan – is unusual. You wouldn't choose these for daywear. They're kid leather – very thin and soft – presumably for bicycling.

"So now we have it: The final, sad moments of Louis La Rothière, spy, murderer, and *agent provocateur*. It begins, I believe, at the station – He meets someone on the platform. The key is of a type used in private deposit boxes. Martin's Bank is on Lombard Steet. Let us say that our man collects *something* from a fellow agent at the station, then deposits it at the nearby bank.

"At some point, he is attacked – suddenly and viciously. He has no time, or is too injured, to put on his gloves. He flees the scene, using a bicycle to affect a speedy escape. Let us imagine his pursuer manages to follow him, for why else would La Rothière work so hard at losing himself in the City's backstreets? How long, Watson, do you think it would take for strychnine to begin to have its effect?"

"It would depend on the dose, but at least fifteen to twenty minutes."

"Yes! Yes!" Holmes exclaimed, "the timing works. He cycles furiously for fifteen to twenty minutes. He reaches Regent's Street, already beginning to slow, to feel the effects of the poison that's entered his system through the cuts on his hands. He's beginning to get clumsy, uncoordinated. Remember the bruises on his calves – from where his feet have repeatedly slipped off the pedals. They continue to spin, hitting him on the leg.

"Lord, he must have been as strong as a horse to have made it so far. If Mr. Brown was correct, by now he's lost his pursuers, but the game isn't over. It isn't unreasonable for him to think that whoever is pursuing him wants what he's collected. Spotting the backdoor of the Polytechnic, he makes one last, Herculean effort. The key is in his hand – He's looking, perhaps, for a safe place to hide it. Somewhere no one would ever think of looking. Maybe in the innards of a New Kingdom princess? We'll never know for sure, for it's there that he exits this world, exclaiming not *'tué'* or *'metuee'*, but *'Il m'a tué'. He has killed me.*"

"But that's horrible!" I cried. La Rothière may have been a foreign agent, but it was hard not to be shocked as Holmes outlined the last moments of a man's life in such pitiful detail.

"It is horrible. And the use of poison on the blade suggests a deliberate assassination. Whoever did this wasn't interested in retrieving what was taken, for with La Rothière dead, whatever was hidden would stay hidden. No, nether England nor 'England's friends' are to blame here. If I had to point the finger, it would be to Russia. Remember the cologne? And France's growing influence over the Tzar isn't approved of by everyone. But I'm sure my brother will be better informed of these things than I am, and able to take the appropriate action."

There was little left for Holmes and me to do, save make our report to Mycroft – by way of a detour to Martin's Bank, where we retrieved a large bundle of papers that, we were assured, "England's friends will be delighted to know are safe."

Soon we were digesting the day's events back in the comfort of Baker Street.

Once more, the drapes were drawn, the fire was lit, and with our pipes well-packed, it felt as though all was well with the world once again.

My friend looked especially thoughtful in the flickering half light. "What are you thinking?" I asked, companionably.

"I think," Holmes said, throwing me a wry smile, "that I'm very happy that Egyptians don't come over to England to dig up our royalty and banquet on their remains."

NOTES

• Watson's editor, Sir Arthur Conan Doyle, was a medical doctor, and appeared to have also been familiar with Dr. Winter. The gentleman appears in one of Conan Doyle's narratives, "Behind the Times".

• The violated grave refers to the practice of grave robbing, which was used to supply medical students with bodies for dissection. After the Anatomy Act of 1832, unclaimed bodies were made available for medical use, effectively putting the grave robbers out of work. However, the Act was hugely controversial as it particularly impacted the poor. Many Victorians, who believed in the literal resurrection of the body, feared that their relatives would be denied salvation because they would not be buried whole.

• The stethoscope was invented in France in 1816.

• Louis Pasteur published his *Germ Theory* in 1861. This was a turning point in modern medicine. Pasteur argued that microbes in the air caused decay, and not the air itself, as was commonly believed.

• Although photographs began to appear in newspapers in the mid-1800's, they were barely legible until the development of the half-tone reproduction process in the 1890's. Many papers therefore still used etchings, where illustrations were required.

• In the Victorian era, "cosmetics" referred to anything medicinal that was applied to the skin. Embellishments were pastes, powders, and paints, which were used to alter the appearance.

• Although *autopsy* is the term used today, there was a great deal of disagreement in the Victorian era about exactly what word should be used to describe the process. *Autopsia* (autopsy), *post-mortem, sectio cadaveris* (dissection of a dead body), *necropsia*, and *necroscopy* were variously used, until autopsy was finally adopted. It should be noted that the term *necropsy* is now used exclusively for animal *post-mortems*, but the word did not have that meaning in Watson's time.

• While Watson doesn't finish the story of Sir John Sirwell's gaul stone, Conan Doyle does. In "Behind the Times", he describes how Winter, having witnessed a young doctor cut into Sir John, only to find no gaul stone, provided one from his own pocket: *"It's always well to bring one in your waistcoat pocket,"* said he with a chuckle, *"but I suppose you youngsters are above all that."*

• Egyptomania did indeed include public "unwrapping parties". However unsavory and disrespectful this may seem, the term "party" is slightly misleading. These events were more like public lectures, and neither especially wild nor, indeed, party-ish. The best-known mummy unroller was a surgeon and antiquary, Thomas Pettigrew, whose lectures and public unwrappings were very popular and highly regarded by the scientific community.

• Alarming as it may seem, *mummia* was taken and prescribed regularly until the 1700's, and was still available as a medicine until 1924. Mummia originally referred to a type of bituminous resin, used in the embalming process, which has antiseptic properties. This resin was used throughout the ancient world. When supplies began to run short in the 1800's, mummia slowly morphed from the resin used to embalm mummies to whole or powdered mummy flesh. After Egypt banned the gruesome trade, European apothecaries began using the corpses of criminals, whose bodies were left to dry in the sun, after execution, before being ground into powder.

• Brummell refers to the royal fashionista, Beau Brummell, who died in 1840.

• The term *namby-pamby*, meaning weak, ineffective, and maudlin, was coined by the poet Henry Carey (1687-1743), who used it as a mocking nickname for fellow poet Ambrose Philips.

• The incidents that Winter ascribes to the cursed mummy closely match stories told about the so-called "*Unlucky Mummy*". The mummy's strikingly beautiful wooden sarcophagus can currently be seen in the British Museum. Interestingly, the whereabouts of the mummy that the sarcophagus once contained are unknown.

• In 1876, Robert Koch proved that a bacterium caused anthrax. This brought an end to the miasma theory.

• The Orloff Special Cologne was created in 1890 for Russia's Prince Orloff. When the fragrance was re-launched by British perfumers, Floris, they renamed it *Special 127* after the page in their "Specials" formula book. Special 127 was Winston Churchill's favourite cologne.

• In the 1880's, relations between France and Imperial Russia were strained by the competing colonial aspirations of both nations. However, relations gradually improved, as France began to see Russia as the only ally who could stand up against Britain. At the start of the 1890's, Russia received a number of large loans from France which brought the allies even closer. However, the loans shifted the balance of power, and some believed that the Tzar was then too reliant on France.